A book flew at his head—

and sailed through him, bouncing off the wall and landing on the floor.

Mouth agape, the woman stared from him to the book and back to him again. "You're a ghost."

"Not exactly. Shall we start over?" He leaned against the wall and folded his arms across his chest. "After a hundred years of being invisible to everyone except *you*, I'd like to know who you are and what you're doing here."

"Of course. Why not? Could today get any weirder?" She sank into the desk chair, shook her head, and sighed. "My name is Tallulah Thompson. I'm a hotel inspector, hired by the current owner as a consultant to find out why the renovations are delayed and what he needs to do to fix it. He's teetering on the brink of bankruptcy."

"What tribe are you?"

She jerked her head up and those doggone lapis lazuli eyes of hers sparked as if she'd strike him with lightning and kill him with one look. "No one asks that. It's not politically correct."

"Well, I guess you haven't been talking to the right people. And I don't know what you mean by that last part. I've never been involved in politics."

"Nowadays, it's considered rude to ask about another person's national origins." She threw her hands up. "Why am I giving a *ghost* an etiquette lesson? What am I thinking?"

Praise for Sharon Buchbinder

"Ms. Buchbinder weaves ancient secrets and modern mysteries into a beautifully written story that will keep you turning the pages."

~USA Today Bestselling Author, Roz Lee

~*~

"Sharon Buchbinder's writing grabs hold from the very first page and stays with you long after the last page been read. Her skill in combining historical fact with suspenseful fiction creates an exciting and dramatic backdrop for her stories. Ms. Buchbinder's books are now on my must-buy list."

~Jennifer Lynne, bestselling author of Gods of Love

The Haunting of Hotel LaBelle

by

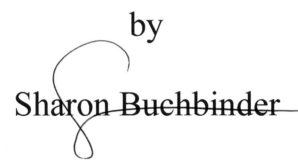

Sharon ~~Buchbinder~~

The Haunting of Hotel LaBelle

Cover Art by *Rae Monet, Inc. Design*

The Wild Rose Press, Inc.
PO Box 708
Adams Basin, NY 14410-0708
Visit us at www.thewildrosepress.com

Publishing History
First Fantasy Rose Edition, 2016
Print ISBN 978-1-5092-1153-1
Digital ISBN 978-1-5092-1154-8

Published in the United States of America

Dedications

This book is dedicated with love to
my husband, Dale,
our son, Joshua,
our daughter-in-law, Elyse,
and our grandson, Dexter.
They remind me every day that family ties
bind with love and priceless memories.
~*~

It is also dedicated to my tireless
and supportive editor,
Amanda Barnett,
who believes in my work
and helps me grow with each manuscript.
~*~

And to Sharon Saracino,
my patient critique partner,
who sticks with me through my ups and downs
and who props me up
and cheers me on when words fail me.

Author's Note

Anyone who has read my previous novels knows that before I begin to write, I conduct extensive research and steep myself in the materials. This approach enables me to speak through the characters and narrative with rich and correct content. I also rely on subject matter experts and beta readers from diverse disciplines and cultural backgrounds who provide corrections and feedback to me before I submit a story for consideration for publication. I would be remiss if I did not thank my readers here, starting with my ever patient husband, Dale Buchbinder, who read every single draft of the story.

My deep gratitude goes to the following people for their expertise and feedback: Toni Chiazza Diblasi, Christy Dixon, Sherri Denora, Amy Dore, Hal Dorin, Karen and Ken Giek, Ernest and Toni Goetling, Nancy Greenwald, Erin Hayes, Penny Nichols, Sharon Saracino, Nancy H. Shanks, Fred and Robin Vandenbroeck, Sonia Vitale-Richardson, Beth White Werrell, and Susan Willis. Big hugs to my brilliant editor, Amanda Barnett, who prunes the thorns from my roses.

Thanks to the hard work of Frank B. Linderman in the late 1920s, the world has a written history of the Absaalooke, or Crow Nation, a traditionally oral culture. As a young man, Linderman became entranced with the West and moved out there to become a hunter and trapper. Over time, Native Americans befriended him and began to tell their stories to him in sign language and through interpreters. The Crows called him the Great Sign Talker and Pretty Shield said he made books speak. Almost a century later, his work crackles with life and takes the reader on breathtaking journeys into another world and another time. If you have not read his books and are interested in Native American stories, biographies, and autobiographies, here are my takes on where you should begin:

I recommend beginning with *Pretty Shield: Medicine Woman of the Crows* and *Plenty-Coups: Chief of the Crows*. Pretty Shield's granddaughter, Alma Hogan Snell, offers us more contemporary perspectives with her books, *Grandmother's Grandchild: My Crow Indian Life* and *A Taste of Heritage: Crow Indian Recipes and Herbal Medicines*.

I hope you enjoy the story. If you are interested in additional sources I used to research this novel, I would be happy to send you my list of references. Just email me at: sharonbellbuchbinder@gmail.com

Happy reading!
Sharon Buchbinder

Prologue

After five years of hard work, scrimping and saving, today Lucius Stewart's dream became reality. This afternoon, he paid the Cattleman's Bank off in full, and now held the deed to the beautiful Hotel LaBelle in his hand. He sat at his desk, sipped an exceptional whiskey from his bar, and dangled a fine cigar between his lips. He liked it when all the patrons and staff were in bed, asleep. During the evening in the crowded bar, with the piano player pounding the keys, it was impossible to even hear his own thoughts.

Lucius blew a smoke ring and stared at the wood ceiling of his office. A good day. Perhaps the best of his thirty-five years of life. Though born and raised in New York City, the West had always called to him. When his mother died, he sold the family home and headed to Big Sky Country. During the ten years of working his way up to general manager in a large hotel in the city, he dreamed of building his own place. He wanted something for city folks like himself who hankered after a taste of the frontier—with the civilized amenities of a soft bed, fine dining, and good wine.

If he'd been married, he would be celebrating with his wife. But the woman he loved turned him down, saying it would never work. In her nation, the women owned the home and all the family possessions. When a man and woman married, the husband moved into the wife's home. And therein lay the rub. They came from different worlds. To keep the Hotel LaBelle up and running, he had to be present, pure and simple. The place wouldn't run itself. Lucius knew if he blinked too long the barkeep would water the liquor, the cowboys would tear the place apart, and the hotel would be destroyed.

So, he decided they were getting married, and *she* was moving in with *him*. They *had* to, especially with a little one on the way. An awful thought sprang into his mind. What if something happened to him before he could convince her his way was the *right* way? Life was unpredictable. Hadn't his father died when he was a small child? If his father hadn't provided for his mother, Lord only knew what his life would have been like growing up. Lucius set the deed to the hotel aside, picked up a pen, dipped it into the inkwell, and began to write.

****

An hour later, satisfied with his work, he dropped the pen on the desk. As soon as the ink dried, he'd put the second document in his safe place, along with the deed. Right now, he was plumb beat. He leaned back in his chair, closed his eyes, and drifted off to sleep.

"Lucius Stewart!"

He fell backward, hitting the chair and his head on the wall. He rubbed the back of his skull and searched for the source of the voice.

"Who's there? What do you want? I don't have any money—I took it all to the bank today."

An old woman stepped out of the shadows. She

wore a buckskin dress covered in elk teeth. Eagle feathers perched on her head as if about to take flight. Anger creased her tanned face.

"Beautiful Blackfeather." The mother of the woman he loved stood before him, the feathers on her head trembling, and her face twisted in rage. "What's wrong? Why are your arms bleeding? What happened to your hair? Is Mourning Dove not well?"

Shaking from head to toe, his heart thundered in his chest like a bear trapped in a cage. All the traditional signs of mourning were right there in front of him, but he refused to believe his eyes. No, it couldn't be. His vision blurred and he wailed. "No, no, tell me it isn't so. Tell me Mourning Dove lives, please!"

"Do not speak of my daughter, you worthless dog," she spoke in Crow at the same time her hands flew in Plains Indian hand talk so fast and with such fury, he could barely keep up.

"Slow down," he signed back. "What is wrong?"

"You. You are what's wrong. You lay with so many women, you thought my daughter was another to toss aside. Now there is a child and you are not man enough to make things right."

"That's not true!" Lucius jumped to his feet. "I love your daughter. I want to marry her. Here in my hotel, with a judge. Make it legal in the eyes of Montana law and white folks. Show her she's worth more to me than a bride price of a horse."

"Liar," Beautiful Blackfeather signed. "You love and leave all women. You hurt many and will do it no more."

"No, no, no. You don't understand. I don't want

any other women." Exasperated, he withdrew a gold wedding band from his pocket and held it out for Beautiful to see. "For Mourning Dove."

She pulled her medicine stick out of her belt and aimed it at his face. A wispy white feather hung on the tip and moved with his breath. She spoke in Crow. Though difficult to understand, Lucius knew enough of the language to recognize she cursed him. Beautiful Blackfeather wasn't any ordinary mother-in-law to be. The Crow considered her the most powerful Medicine Woman in Montana. He had to stop her, make her comprehend his intentions.

The room spun, colors twisted and whirled like a kaleidoscope, and his fingers and toes tingled. He grabbed the edge of the desk and squeezed his eyes shut to maintain his balance as the floor shifted. He opened them to discover Beautiful Blackfeather was gone. When he raised his hands to wipe away the sweat soaking his face, his stomach hit the floor. His hands had disappeared too.

Chapter One

Billings, Montana, Present Day

Tallulah Thompson stood inside the largest of the caves in Pictograph Cave State Park. She focused her binoculars on the distant figures painted thousands of years ago by hunters who camped out in the protected space. Alone in the room, she scanned the walls—then dropped the field glasses in astonishment. A tall, tanned man with two long black braids stood with his back to her. Wearing buckskin moccasins, pants, and a breech cloth, he pressed a stick to the wall. Stroking with great concentration, the man focused on his drawing, and the muscles in his back rippled. The small figure of a turtle emerged from his work. *He must be participating in one of the interpretive events the park noted on the website. Great idea. But he should know better than to touch the walls.* Just as she was about to call out to the man, a noisy group entered the space. She glanced at the family of five and turned back to the actor—but he had disappeared.

She searched the cavern. *Where could he have gone? Maybe there was a back exit?* A few moments later, on the walk to the visitor center, she mulled over the disappearing man. She hated to be a tattletale, but those walls were national treasures and shouldn't be marred, even by a well-intentioned employee. She found the friendly park ranger with the beard and wire-rimmed glasses rubbing Tallulah's chubby dog's belly.

"Thanks so much for keeping an eye on Franny so I could see the caves."

He handed her the leash. "No problem. She's been greeting every guest."

"Looking for food, no doubt. Pugs live to eat."

The park ranger whispered into the dog's velvety ears. "What happens at the park, stays at the park."

Franny snorted and licked his nose.

Tallulah hated to break up the light moment, but she had to say *something,* the paintings in the caves were priceless. "I hate to be the bearer of bad news."

He placed the dog on the ground and stood. "Uh-oh. Someone leave trash in the caves? Climb over the fence? Take a rock?" He shook his head. "It's a nuisance, but my job, I'll go talk to whoever did it. What do they look like?"

"Someone was *drawing* on the walls. It was your interpreter, the guy in the Native American costume working in the Pictograph Cave."

The ranger's brow furrowed. "We don't have any events going on in the caves, or on the grounds for that matter. I have no idea who you're talking about."

"Tall, extremely tan, long black braids. I didn't see his face."

The ranger shook his head. "Nope, nobody like that here today. The only guy who works here who *might* fit the description is visiting his sick aunt on the Crow Reservation."

Then who had she seen in the cave?

"My imagination must have been in overdrive." Her face flushed. "Sorry I bothered you." She scooped up the pug. "Thanks again for taking care of Franny." She hightailed it to her rental vehicle before she made an even bigger fool of herself.

Why was this happening now? She hadn't had visions this vivid since her mother and father died and she went to live with her grandmother.

Her grandmother warned her about her gift. Told her to keep it to herself or suffer the same consequences as her mother. Tallulah tried, but occasionally she used her second sight on the sly to help a few of her clients. Sometimes a pesky earthbound spirit needed to be guided to its next destination. But, this one—he was so *real.* The strength of the apparition took her by surprise. She hadn't even *suspected* he wasn't real. That was one *powerful* sacred space, strong enough to suck her back in time to see the artist who created the stick figures on the cave walls.

She leaned back against the headrest of the SUV, closed her eyes, and took deep, cleansing breaths. Her grandmother would have scolded Tallulah for telling the park ranger what she saw.

"He's not one of us," she would have said. "You should *never* share your visions with anyone you don't know well. They'll think you're crazy, try to lock you up, drug you."

Like her mother.

Except she hadn't initially realized the artist was a vision. She rubbed the turquoise talisman her grandmother had given her for protection, and a sense of peace flowed over her. Tallulah opened her eyes, stared through the glass sunroof, and admired the cloud formation that appeared to be painted on a huge blue canvas. It looked like an eagle, its huge white wings outstretched.

Big Sky Country, indeed.

The apparition in the cave put her on notice. *Be prepared.* You are on special lands, as sacred as her grandmother's home in the Choctaw Nation in Durant, Oklahoma.

The lengthening shadows on the craggy hillside told her it was time to buckle up and face what was certain to be a distressed property and a distraught hotel owner. She checked her dog's safety restraint, then started the engine. "Time to work for our keep, Franny."

The fawn pug cocked her head, stuck her tongue out, and appeared terribly interested in her owner's words.

"You know what we have to do, right? Get in, get it fixed, and get out. Time is money and while we love to rescue hotels, the more time we spend there, the less money we make." And the lower her bank account dropped. She wasn't starving, but if she didn't keep moving ahead like a shark, she and Franny might be fighting over her expensive dog food. And she couldn't count on her visions to put dog or people food on the table.

After earning a Master of Management in Hospitality from one of the best universities in the country, and steady advancement in New York City hotels for over a decade, Tallulah knew what did and didn't work. During her education, she learned the business of managing a hotel from marketing to profit margins. Her internship and employment provided the nitty-gritty of the real world. She'd cleaned toilets, hauled bags up to rooms, registered guests, and served food. Hotel management was a twenty-four hours a day, seven days a week business. She kept in touch with her classmates and knew the industry ate half of them alive.

The grueling hours, the demanding clients, and the constant budget pressures weren't easy, especially for women who wanted families. Some, like her friend, a superb pastry chef and hotel manager, had left the field completely, choosing a forty-hour work week. Now she was an elementary school principal with a handsome husband who coached the basketball team, and a tiny army of her own adorable little ones.

Instead of opting out of the hotel world, Tallulah stayed in the game by starting her own consulting business. Granted, she wasn't a millionaire TV celebrity like that bald guy who went around the country inspecting hotels, but she made ends meet. Maybe they didn't overlap, but they did touch. Last year, she and the IRS agreed that her company, T & F Hotel Inspectors, Inc., was truly a going concern. Her spare bedroom in her small, well-organized—well maybe she was a *tad* crazy about sticky notes— Trenton, New Jersey apartment served as her business address.

Most days she commuted to work in her pajamas, saving on gas and wardrobe costs. Her coworker, Franny, was pleasant and not terribly gabby, except when she was hungry or needed to go out. Best of all, as her own boss, she determined the work hours. She traveled at the client's expense, and her black marker, pads of sticky notes, and Franny, the "F" in T & F Hotel Inspectors, *always* went with her.

She now exited the winding, pine-tree-flanked road onto I90 West, to search for her newest client's establishment, the historic Hotel LaBelle. Established in the early 1900s, the hotel had been one of the first in the area to provide fine dining and sleeping accommodations for travelers who wanted the adventure of the Wild West, without the discomfort. The current owner emailed her after reading one of her guest posts on a large travel website about the challenges of modernizing historic hotels.

Dear Ms. Thompson,

I am writing to see if you can assist me with my historic hotel. I purchased it at an auction for the price of back taxes, which came to over three hundred thousand dollars. Abandoned by the owner in 1905, the Hotel LaBelle was ahead of its time for the era. Everything inside was made from the finest materials, so even though it has been unattended, beneath the animal droppings and graffiti, I could see her beauty. I was in love.

I obtained a bank loan for a million dollars to restore the original property. My plan was to get the dining room up and running first, along with five of the original rooms. The earnings from the restaurant and the rooms were supposed to help with the costs of renovation and expanding the hotel, as there is plenty of land. Over the last year, I have begun to question my decision and my sanity. There have been so many problems with the help and with construction. Customers are fleeing, not flocking to stay here. I am on the verge of bankruptcy.

Can you help me? I have enough money set aside to pay your fee and travel expenses. Please say you will come. I am desperate.

Yours truly,

William Wellington, III
Owner and General Manager
Hotel LaBelle

A million dollar budget intrigued her. How could she refuse? She'd never been to Montana. And Will, or WWIII as she liked to think of him, hadn't balked at her price or her terms, including bringing Franny. The GPS directed her to continue on Interstate 90W, skirting the town. At the Yellowstone River, she found a dilapidated sign and the dirt road leading to her destination.

"Oh, baby, I think the owner has some 'splaining to do. That sign is awful. And how are you supposed to get down a dirt road in bad weather." She shook her head and jotted a note on her ever-present yellow sticky pad. "Good thing we have a four-wheel drive."

Franny, too short to see over the dashboard, was spared the sight of the run-down wraparound porch, tires serving as planters for bedraggled flowers, and a rusty pickup truck parked in the middle of the driveway. The place looked like a junk dealer's lot. All that was missing was a barking dog chained to a post.

"This is even worse than I imagined. Hotel LaHelle would be a better name. Maybe he hasn't seen us yet. We can just back up and—"

A middle-aged man with a ponytail, leather vest, a paunch that drooped over his jeans, and cowboy boots bounded out the front door. He tripped down the steps, righted himself, and shoved his head through her open window.

"Ms. Thompson? Aren't you a pretty little lady? What a sight for sore eyes! Welcome to Hotel LaBelle!"

Personal space was obviously a foreign concept for her new client. She leaned away from the close talker, his garlic-laced breath, and his unwelcome compliments. "You must be Mr. Wellington. Please, allow me to get out and do a walk around the grounds with my dog."

He yanked the car door open. "Of course, let me get your bag and take it to your room. When you're ready, come on in and we'll have a beer."

"Coffee, please. I never drink while I'm working." Her instincts screamed, *this guy is bad news!* But her checking account yelled, *you spent the money already!* She grabbed her bag, sticky notes, and pug. "See you in thirty minutes."

The further away she got from the owner, the better she felt. Her muscles, knotted in a fight or flight response, relaxed as she walked along the winding river and gazed at the islands dotting the water. A startled wild turkey gobbled and flapped his wings at the little dog. Unaware that she was half the size of the bird, Franny raced after him, her curly little tail wagging, stopping only when Tallulah tugged on the leash.

"That's enough excitement for you today."

The river view and surrounding lands were the saving grace for this hotel. Make that a positive sticky note. She had to give him some good feedback along with the bad. Front and back, the exterior, the curbside appeal, if you will, had all the charm of a hillbilly hideout, without the handsome hillbilly. She would need to set some very strong boundaries with Wellington—who could very well be nicknamed Smellington at this point. *Yuck.*

Reluctance dragging at every step, she climbed the

front stairs, entered the structure, and gasped.

The long, smooth registration desk appeared to be made of highly polished mahogany, as did the walls and ceiling. Carvings of trees, waterways, and mountains rose across the surface of every wall. Peeking between the trees were deer and turkeys. Fish leaped out of the river and clouds scudded over the mountains. Turning in a slow circle, Tallulah absorbed the genteel grandeur of the lobby. Well, this was getting a lot better, she thought as she jotted more positive notes.

Next to the gleaming wooden stairs, metal lattice work surrounded a wooden box that comprised the elaborate cage elevator. On the second floor, railings on three sides formed a gallery from which the rooms' occupants could view the entire lobby. Just as she completed her slow circuit and note taking, a woman with long dark braids exited a hotel room, a cleaning basket in one hand and a vacuum in the other. She needed to interview that woman and any other staff Wellington had on site.

"See anything you like?" The owner appeared in front of her and waggled his eyebrows. Tallulah hoped he wasn't referring to himself. "Sure you don't want something stronger than coffee?"

She tucked the notes into her purse. "Mr. Wellington—"

"Please, call me Will." He grinned, exposing crooked yellow teeth. One more strike in a growing list of unappealing pitches. "As in, where there's a Will, there's a way."

Okay, time for the talk.

"Mr. Wellington, please behave in a professional manner with me."

His face fell. "I'm sorry. I was just trying to be friendly."

"Friendly is a handshake and a polite hello, not leering at me or wiggling your eyebrows."

At the top of the stairs, the maid burst out laughing. "I told him not to pull that crap on you. Would he listen? No. Thinks he's a ladies' man like the original owner, 'Love 'Em and Leave 'Em Lucius.' "

Tallulah looked up at the woman. "And you are?"

"Emma Horserider."

"Ms. Horserider—"

"Emma is just fine." She grinned displaying even white teeth.

"Okay, I see. I'm Tallulah Thompson. Mr. Wellington called me in to help him save his hotel. I'm only here for a week. I would love to chat with you."

Emma shot the owner a hard look. "Happy to do it—just not now and not here."

Tallulah was dying to hear the backstory on this one. "Good, you tell me when and where, and I'll meet you."

Emma nodded. "You ever been to Little Big Horn?"

"No, this is my first trip to Montana."

"There's a restaurant, a trading post really, just outside the park. You can't miss it. A huge arrow points to it. I'll meet you there tomorrow at noon." Emma turned to Wellington. "If you really want to save this place, you need to behave. This woman is here to help you. Sit down, shut up, and listen." Emma stomped out the front door.

"Ms. Thompson, can we start over?"

"Yes, let's try, shall we?"

He extended his hand. "My name is Will, and I really need your help. I'm sorry I acted like a jerk. I do that when I get anxious. Right now, I'm about to have a nervous breakdown. Can I get you a cup of coffee?"

She took his hand and gave it a firm shake. "Nice to meet you, Will. I'm here to help you save Hotel LaBelle. I would love a cup of coffee and a bite to eat, if you have something simple."

An hour and two delicious buffalo burgers later—one half for Franny—Will sat with his head in his hands. "I just don't know what to do. Emma is a hardworking woman, but she refuses to clean some of the rooms, says they have a spirit wandering in them. The construction workers are good—when they work. They have a habit of up and walking off the job if they hear of better paying work elsewhere, even though I have a contract with the company. The hotel is on the grid, but the power goes out often in the winter. I'm going to have to invest in an emergency generator. Each room has a fireplace, but some of the rooms are freezing, even when the fire is roaring. And, every now and again, I find wild animals wandering through the place."

Tallulah pulled out her sticky notepad. "Wild animals?"

"Turkeys, deer, even a mountain goat one time." He shook his head and stood up to clear the coffee cups. "I lock up every night, and in the morning, I find doors flapping in the wind. If I believed in ghosts, I'd say this place is haunted."

A chill ran down Tallulah's back. "What about your guests? What do they say?"

"The last guests I had were a couple of guys who

fished all day, drank all night, and trashed the room. Supposed to stay a week. Ran out in the middle of the third night and didn't pay their bill."

"What happened?"

"I have no idea. All I know is, even after repeated cleanings, their room still smells like dead fish."

What would send two tough guys running for the hills?

She had to find out or she wouldn't be helping the guy. "Will, what room do you have me in?"

"The best one in the house. The honeymoon suite. Claw-foot bathtub, king-sized bed, in room bar."

"Were your fishing guests in that room?"

He looked horrified. "Absolutely not."

"I want to stay in the same room they stayed in."

"Naw, you don't want that. There's still a faint smell of fish in the closet."

"I insist. It's time for me to fish or cut bait." She smiled. "Humor me."

He shook his head. "Okay, but don't say I didn't warn you about the stink."

It's not the odor I'm worried about.

An hour later, after a guided tour of the hotel upstairs and down, and taking the pug out for her bedtime constitutional, Tallulah admired her room. The updated bathroom, two queen-sized beds, and flat-screen TV brought the place into contemporary times, but the carved wood-paneled walls spoke of its rich history.

Every muscle in her body screamed for a hot bath. Tallulah cranked on the faucets of the claw-foot tub, plugged her cell phone in to charge, and stripped out of her travel clothes. She stepped into the steaming water and sank down into the bubbles, closing her eyes with a sigh of contentment. Franny plopped on the rug next to the tub and snored. An hour later, Tallulah awoke to a yapping pug and tepid bathwater. She stepped over the dancing dog, dropped her flannel nightgown over her head, and brushed her teeth while the little beast cocked her head and watched.

"Let it never be said that a pug allowed its owner to brush their teeth alone."

Franny snorted.

The nightlight cast a small yellow glow when Tallulah opened the bathroom door, headed to the bed—and stopped. A drop-dead gorgeous mustachioed man with brown wavy hair falling to the collar of his old-fashioned suit perched on the edge of her four poster. The scent of cigar smoke and whiskey wafted to her on the breeze from the overhead fan, and his shadow stretched across the quilt in an extended parody of his height.

Franny leaped at the man's legs and barked. He reached down to pet the dog, murmured something, and she wagged her curly little tail.

Rooted to the spot, heart thrumming in her throat, Tallulah debated running back into the bathroom and calling Will on her cell phone to get his butt up to the room and explain how this stranger got past her dead bolted and chained door. She took a deep breath. Flight wasn't an option since he blocked her path from the room. Besides, she'd have to unwrap her pug from around his ankles or leave her here with the intruder. Not a chance.

Time to put up a good fight.

"Who the hell are you?" She wanted to snatch

Franny away from him, but didn't want to get too close to this stranger. "What are you doing in my room?"

The man's dark, intelligent eyes widened and his eyebrow quirked. "You can see me?"

"Of course I can see you. I repeat. Who the hell are you? You're sitting on my bed as if you own the place."

"I'm Lucius Stewart. I do own the place. I'm the proprietor of Hotel LaBelle."

Chapter Two

Hotel LaBelle, Billings, Montana, Present Day

The long, white flannel nightgown did little to hide the shapely figure of the woman with the wild blonde hair and wide blue eyes. Lucius Stewart found her womanly charms incredibly distracting but remained startled beyond belief—she could actually see him. *Really see him. How was it possible?*

"Is this some kind of joke? Hazing the hotel consultant? Tell Will it isn't funny, and get out of my room. *Now*."

She pointed toward the door, her white-tipped fingernail reminding him of the breath feather on the tip of Beautiful Blackfeather's medicine stick. He inspected her face, his gaze traveling slowly over her pouty red lips and her cheekbones. He inspected her longer than any civilized woman would deem polite. She glared back at him, fists on her hips—just like someone else he'd known years ago.

Her mannerisms, regal bearing, and commanding presence sucker punched him, turning his limbs to jelly and his mouth to mush. If he believed in reincarnation like he'd heard some of the Alaskan tribes did, he'd say she was Mourning Dove reborn with blonde hair and blue eyes. He let out a long breath and managed to untie his tongue.

"You Crow?"

Her frown became deeper, her voice angrier. "Excuse me?"

Perhaps she didn't understand him. He spoke slower and louder, "Your tribe. Are. You. Crow?"

"I. Am. Not. Deaf." She patted her thigh. "Franny come. Get away from him."

The little dog with the pushed-in face and bug eyes jumped and wagged its curly little tail harder as if in defiance of her owner's orders. *What's with this so-ugly-it's-cute creature, anyway?*

"Franny! Come *here*." The little dog plopped on its haunches and looked back and forth between the disturbingly familiar woman and him as if trying to decide which way to go.

Lucius stood and stretched, still trying to reconcile this woman's ability to see him and her uncanny resemblance to the woman he'd loved and lost.

"Don't you come near me." She backed up to the desk, hands scrabbling on the mahogany surface. "Or I'll, I'll—"

"What? Hit me?" He laughed at her surprised expression—the mirror image of Mourning Dove's wide-eyed, open-mouthed look when he'd proposed to her. "Throw something at me. Please." He almost hoped he'd get smacked so he could feel *something*. Anything was better than this nothingness. A book flew at his head—and sailed through him, bouncing off the wall and landing on the floor.

Mouth agape, the woman stared from him to the book and back to him again. "You're a ghost."

"Not exactly. Shall we start over?" He leaned against the wall and folded his arms across his chest.

"After a hundred years of being invisible to everyone except *you*, I'd like to know who you are and what you're doing here."

"Of course. Why not? Could today get any weirder?" She sank into the desk chair, shook her head, and sighed. "My name is Tallulah Thompson. I'm a hotel inspector, hired by the current owner as a consultant to find out why the renovations are delayed and what he needs to do to fix it. He's teetering on the brink of bankruptcy."

"What tribe are you?"

She jerked her head up and those doggone lapis lazuli eyes of hers sparked as if she'd strike him with lightning and kill him with one look. "No one asks that. It's not politically correct."

"Well, I guess you haven't been talking to the right people. And I don't know what you mean by that last part. I've never been involved in politics."

"Nowadays, it's considered rude to ask about another person's national origins." She threw her hands up. "Why am I giving a *ghost* an etiquette lesson? What am I thinking?"

"The Crow gal who cleans this place can feel me but never hears or sees me. You can. How is that possible?"

Tallulah wrapped her arms around her shoulders and shuddered as if chilled. "I'm Choctaw. My grandmother is a Medicine Woman. I see…things."

"I *knew* you had Indian blood." The cheekbones sealed the deal for him.

"Native American."

"What?"

"The proper terminology these days is Native

21

American. And it's genes, not blood."

"You just gotta correct everything I say, don't you? Here's another rude question for you. Why are you blonde? In my day, only the painted ladies changed their hair color."

"Oh. My. God. You just don't stop, do you? Okay, okay, you win." She shook her head. "This is my *real* hair color. My grandfather was a German immigrant who went to Oklahoma for the land lotteries, met and married my grandmother, and had a mess of kids. My mother married a nice German man, then they both died in a car accident, and my grandmother raised me. Happy now?"

"Yes. Thank you. Was that so hard?"

She glared at him. "What about you? Why are you still hanging around here? Don't you have a long, dark tunnel to go into and a light to follow?"

"What?" He had no idea what she was talking about. There were no tunnels in Hotel LaBelle, and the only lights were the ones he installed a century ago. "You sure do speak in riddles."

"Since we've dispensed with being polite, I'm just going to lay it out for you. You're dead. You don't belong here. It's time for you to move on." She pointed to the ceiling. "Heaven awaits you. Or, whatever the alternative is."

He sat down heavily on the bed, and the little dog yapped and jumped again. "Let me tell you how I got here." He recounted his last evening in his office and the visit from Beautiful Blackfeather. "She didn't kill me, Ms. Tallulah. She cursed me. I don't know the exact words she used. I don't speak Crow that well. For all I know, I'm stuck here for eternity."

Lips pouted, she stood and reached for a shawl at the foot of the bed, snatched it up, and threw it over her shoulders.

"Don't be afraid. I can't hurt you." He wriggled his fingers. "I can't even pick anything up with these things."

Tallulah settled back into the chair and arranged the shawl over her full breasts. *A pity.* He'd been enjoying the view of her chilled nipples straining against the thin cotton and the tantalizing scent of roses. He recalled the pleasures of a woman's body, and Lord forgive him, this pretty little gal with the luscious lips was causing all sorts of naughty thoughts to run through his mind, like how he'd like to nibble that lovely, tender spot down at the base of her neck and inhale the smell of her sweet body until he got dizzy. Mouth dry, he licked his lips. And paused. Not once in the last century had he felt either hunger or thirst. He felt like a man in a desert—*parched.*

She knotted the shawl, gave it a hard tug, and grasped the turquoise pendant on her neck. "What have you been *doing* all this time?"

No chance of that sliding off her now. *Doggone it.* "At first, it was like I was in a deep sleep. I came to and watched my beautiful hotel slowly fall into ruins. It hurt so much, I tried to leave the place, get away. Can't go out on the grounds. Farthest I can go is the porch. I spend a lot of time there, watching the sun rise and set."

"I can't even imagine," she whispered.

Tallulah's husky voice and her unsettling similarities to Mourning Dove stirred desires buried deep in his heart. He yearned for a human touch and ached with the need to be fully present. For now, he'd have to be satisfied with the fact that this beautiful, vexing woman could see and hear him.

"I've been lonely. No one to talk to, except the animals. They see and hear me, like your little pooch here. What type of dog is that anyway?"

A smile, a real one that went to her eyes, penetrated her serious demeanor. "A pug. Dog of royalty. Originally from China. The Duke and Duchess of Windsor had three and took them to social events with them."

"She sure is ugly." He patted her head and the dog reacted as if she felt him. *Interesting.* "But cute."

"Tell me what it's like to watch a century pass before your eyes."

Her even white teeth nibbled at her lower lip, and he couldn't tear his gaze away from her. "I had a limited view, you know, from the porch. I could see the river and watch the animals come by. A great Medicine Woman once told me the plains used to be black with buffalo. She told me the herds would come down to the river out back, so thick you could walk across the water on their backs, but before I arrived here in 1900, white men hunted them for sport. All these years, I sat on that porch and watched for them, every day. Never saw more than a handful in all that time."

Tallulah shook her head. "They were hunted almost to extinction."

His eyes blurred, and he could barely speak. "Gone? All of them?"

"Not quite. Native Americans protested—a lot. Finally, laws were passed, scientists were called in, and the buffalo population is rising."

He passed a hand over his face. *Funny.* Every other

time he did that, he felt nothing. This time, it was almost as if he touched gauze.

"Why would people kill the food and shelter that supported the Crow and other tribes?"

She shrugged, and the shawl slipped down a notch, exposing her lovely neck a bit more. "Eminent domain? Selfishness? Greed? Arrogance? Ignorance? Cultural disdain? Hatred? Hard to know where to start or end the list."

"A crime. The people responsible for it should be here with me. A hundred years gives you lots of time to think about what you did in your life. I wasn't a devil." He hazarded a smile. "But, I was no angel."

"Well, Lucius-you're-no-angel, I have an important question to ask you." She pursed her full lips and considered him for a moment, as if appraising him and his worth. "Tell me the truth. Are you behind all the problems the new hotel owner is having?"

He jumped to his feet, and her eyes widened.

"The new owner? You mean the thief who stole my life's work away from me and is tearing it apart? He's a no good, rotten scoundrel and has no right to call this place his home. I built it, loved it, took care of it—and he's ripping it apart."

She frowned and shook her head. "Mr. Stewart, the hotel was full of animal droppings, vagrants, and graffiti. The local kids came out here to get high and screw around. He bought it for back taxes and put in a lot of money to clean it up. He's trying very hard and seems quite sincere to me."

He paced the room, running his thumbs under his suspenders. Franny trotted behind at his heels. "The man has no sense of history. Did you see what he's doing? Adding ugly rooms, all shiny white with no wood, no warmth, no heart. Who would want to sleep in a room with nothing but white everywhere and bright lights? That man has put them big, flat, black things on every wall in this hotel. Talking heads, pictures that scream at you, how can you even hear yourself think with all those people yelling at you from the walls? And the bar? Did you see what he did to my bar? He took down all the stuffed animal heads my friends collected specifically for me! Why would he do that?"

"Mr. Stewart—"

"Don't you get all formal with me. I know my rights. This is my hotel. I paid the bank off, and I have the deed."

She shook her head, and the shawl dipped down another inch. "There was no deed found when you went missing, Mr. Stewart."

"Lucius. Call me Lucius. I had the deed the same night I wrote my last will and testament. The night Beautiful Blackfeather cursed me." Rage boiled in his chest. "If I had fingers that worked, I'd get it and show it to you."

"Lucius, I'm very sorry to remind you, but even if you *could* get your hands on the document, you are legally dead."

"I'm not dead. I'm, I'm—" He stopped pacing and threw his hands up in exasperation.

"In limbo. Where only animals and I can see and hear you. Ever since I arrived in Montana, I've been seeing things. If I were to tell people I saw and spoke with you, do you know what would happen to me?"

He shook his head.

"I'd be locked up or drugged until I didn't see you

or any other visions again. My grandmother warned me. She made me swear to keep my second sight to myself, especially among white people."

"Please, I beg of you. Help me save my hotel. She's all I have."

"I'm sorry, Lucius." A tear trickled down her cheek, and she swiped at it. "In a way, I'm trapped in limbo too."

The flame of hope that this amazing woman could set things right for him and undo this wretched curse flickered and blew out. His old friend, grief, overcame him, weighed him down, and pressed him backward into the wall.

"Lucius! What's happening? Where are you?"

He closed his eyes and fell into oblivion.

Chapter Three

Tallulah lunged at the wall, feeling for a telltale edge, a trick lock, something tangible and rational to explain the man's disappearance. Franny barked and yapped, leaping against the wall as if attempting to help her owner. Their efforts failed to reveal a secret passage. She plopped on the edge of the bed, ran her hand over the bumps of the quilt, and inhaled the heady mixture of cigar smoke, whiskey, and man. He seemed so *real*. Vivid and bold. Never before had she experienced a vision quite like Lucius. If he was this big in death, what had he been like in life? She *had* to find out more about him.

First thing in the morning, she was going to ask Will about the new rooms. He never said one word about them. Only an idiot would try to convert a historic hotel like this to an ultra-modern No Tell Motel. *Was Lucius lying to her?* What was she thinking? Ghosts were not reliable informants. They saw things as they were in the past, not as they existed in the present. Then again, the lingering glances the bold-as-brass ghost cast at her were not exactly chaste. She'd put the shawl on when she saw him staring at her chest. The chilly air gave her goose bumps, not the alarmingly dapper spirit with rugged good looks—and dimples that made her feel as if he was thinking naughty thoughts every time he smiled at her.

Enough.

She grabbed a larger sticky notepad out of her briefcase and jotted down a list of things to ask Will in the morning before she left for her meeting with Emma. Of all the hotels she'd been asked to save, this one was turning out to be the most bizarre—and its handsome ghost the most intriguing. She anticipated she would have difficulty sleeping after this curious incident of the good-looking ghost in the night. Franny, on the other hand, was already snoring.

****

Bright and early the next day, after Franny's morning stroll, Tallulah and the pug found the hotelier in the kitchen. He held a cup in one hand and a small newspaper in the other. When they walked in, he stuffed the newsprint into his shirt pocket, poured Tallulah a mug full of hot coffee, and set a bowl of fresh water down for Franny.

"Smells great." She sipped. "Nice and strong, just the way I like it."

"These parts, if your coffee is bad, no one will consider even entering your hotel, much less staying at it." He nodded at the large espresso machine. "We have a top of the line for more exotic offerings."

She pulled out her sticky notes. "I have a few observations and some questions."

He pointed at her and pulled his index finger back. "Shoot."

She picked up a note and handed it to him, starting with the positive feedback as she always did. "You have a beautiful location. The river and all the wildlife give you a tremendous advantage over other hotels."

Will stared at the star on the sticky note and

smiled.

"The lobby and woodworking are stunning. The work and love that went into this hotel when it was built and your restoration of it shine through. It is one of the most unusual and beautiful properties I've had the pleasure to inspect."

"Thank you." He glanced up from the growing pile of starred sticky notes, a broad smile wreathing his face. "You said you had questions?"

"Did you show me all the rooms in the hotel?"

"Ah, you know what? I missed the one under construction." He gave her a sheepish grin. "Figured you didn't need to see the mess."

She studied his expression and wondered if the man really thought she was an idiot. "You have to show me everything, or I can't help you. I thought I made that clear. You must be completely open and honest with me, or I walk."

He glanced around the room, everywhere but at her eyes. He spoke to a spot over her head, "I'm a proud man, Tallulah. This is hard on me."

"It will only get harder, trust me."

She tapped the counter and pointed to her sticky note pile. "I have more of these, with frowny faces, the kind guests make when they have a bad experience at a hotel."

He looked chastened. "I'm sorry. I'll make sure you see everything."

"Good, I'm glad we cleared that up. Do you have photos of the hotel before you began the renovations?"

"Sure. Hold on, I'll be right back."

Will strode out of the room, his cowboy boots clomping on the hardwood floors.

Lucius slid onto the stool Will vacated, causing Tallulah to nearly drop her mug. Franny barked with glee.

"Happy to see you too, little doggy. What's its name?"

"Her name is Franny. What are *you* doing here?" She hissed. "Trying to make me crazy?"

Tanned, rested, and ready, how could a ghost look this good in the bright light of day?

"Who me?" He shrugged. "I love the smell of coffee, don't you?"

Thank God she was fully clothed this time. Alive or dead, Lucius Stewart was much too distracting, with that all-too-knowing twinkle in his eyes that made her feel as if he was about to sweep her into bed. She rubbed her pendant, wishing it would make him disappear. He didn't budge. "Shouldn't you be haunting the attic or porch or basement?"

He grinned, and those damn dimples made her stomach flip. "Now what kinda fun would that be?"

Will clomped back into the kitchen, dropped a three-ring binder on the counter, and sat *through* Lucius—who grimaced in disgust, leaped up, and strode to the espresso machine. The hundred-year-old spirit pretended great interest in all the knobs and dials while Franny rolled over onto her back at his feet. Tallulah tried to focus on the photos and not the spirit who smelled like all the things her grandmother told her to stay away from—cigars, whiskey, and sex.

"This is the original owner, 'Love 'Em and Leave 'Em Lucius.'" A grainy black-and-white photo showed the exact same man currently examining the high-tech coffee maker. In the picture, he held a glass of wine and stood with his foot on the brass rail that ran the length of the bar.

Lucius whispered in her ear. "Not my best photo."

She swatted at her neck, and Will gave her an odd look.

"Fruit fly," she lied. "They follow me wherever I go."

"It's your perfume," Lucius breathed on her neck.

Focus, girl. Will's attentions had been overbearing and annoying. Why did the same behavior from this spirit wreak havoc with her hormones? Did it have something to do with the fact that she could see him and no one else could? She had to ignore that melting feeling in her knees and be professional.

"This here was the bar." Will pointed at the photos. "Everywhere you looked there was some kind of dead animal. Cougar, buffalo, deer, moose, turkeys, pheasants, and jack rabbits. The walls bristled with antlers."

"A few well-placed pieces could add some ambiance to the bar." She flipped the pages. "Right now, it's pretty sterile. Did you keep any of these?"

"Against my better judgment, yeah. Emma insisted the spirit would be angry if I destroyed them." He shook his head and his ponytail flopped back and forth. "Not that I believe in ghosts."

Lucius popped up behind Will. Tallulah snorted into her coffee.

"Sorry." She mopped at the counter with a napkin. "So where is this game collection?"

"In the wine cellar in the basement." He flipped a page. "Not that I have much call for wine. People around here are into micro-brews. I've got all the local flavors on draft."

"That's smart. Have you considered doing any co-promotions with the beer companies?"

He shook his head. "I don't have the best relations with the townspeople."

Lucius nodded vehemently behind Will and said, "Ask him why."

Just what she needed, a ghost coaching her. Hard enough to focus on the work at hand when Lucius was around, much less with him talking to her nonstop.

She tore her gaze away from Lucius. "Why is that? People usually want new places to succeed, especially one with this much history."

He flipped a page of the notebook back and forth and avoided eye contact. "I've run up a few bills."

"How much are you talking about?"

"A couple hundred." His voice trailed off into a mumble.

"A couple hundred dollars? Is that all?"

"Thousand."

"A couple hundred *thousand*?" She jumped to her feet, and Franny yipped. "What happened to the bank loan? Where did it go?"

Will stared at that spot over her head and shrugged.

Lucius mimed riding a horse.

She glanced at the newspaper poking out of Will's shirt pocket. *The newspaper Will had been holding wasn't the Billings Sentine. In fact, it wasn't a newspaper at all—it was a racing sheet.*

Fists on her hips, Tallulah demanded, "Do you have a gambling problem?"

"No." He shook his head so hard his teeth rattled. "I can stop anytime."

Lucius guffawed, startling Franny, making her bug eyes bigger and buggier.

Tallulah grit her teeth. "Will, you have a lot more problems than I can fix." She grabbed her notes and turned on her heel. "I think it's time for me to leave."

"No!" Will and Lucius shouted in unison.

Tears filled Will's eyes. "Please don't go. No more horses, I promise. This place is my biggest gamble. I've lost so much—I *can't* afford to lose it."

Lucius got down on his knees and folded his hands. Franny sat beside him and begged too.

A mixture of anger and pity churned inside her. Never before had a live and a dead man begged her not to leave them—at the same time. She shook her head, and a strangled laugh escaped. "I'm going to regret this, I just know it."

"Thank you!" Will jumped up and down. "Thank you, thank you, thank you!"

Lucius offered her a charming grin and blew her a kiss.

A flock of butterflies quivered in her belly. She shook her head. *I must be nuts.* Of all the ghosts in all of the hotels she'd visited, this one was the most annoying, amusing—and attractive. Franny ran in circles and yelped.

A three ring circus. And she was the only one who could appreciate it.

"Come on, Will. Show me those rooms." She picked up the pug. "Do *not* hide anything else from me."

"Yes, ma'am, right away." He led her up the stairs to the opposite end of the hall from hers and opened the door. "Ta dah! The modern traveler's dream room."

To say the room was institutional would be an understatement. White walls, shiny white shelves, a coat hanging area but no dresser, a low white counter under the flat screen TV, a white table that looked like it belonged in a hospital room, and white towels—folded incorrectly—in a Spartan white-tiled bathroom greeted her. The sawdust and glue made her and Franny sneeze.

Lucius strolled out of the shower. "What did I tell you?"

Tallulah glared at him and put her fingers to her lips. Franny wriggled happily in her arms, and she put the dog on the floor. Lucius patted the pug's belly while Franny rolled in a delirium of ecstasy at his feet. If the pug had been a cat, she would have sworn Lucius was made of catnip.

Damn this man—no, ghost—was getting under her skin.

"Will, who's your decorator?" She wanted to ask if it was someone who specialized in hospitals, but restrained herself.

He puffed up his chest and jabbed at it with his thumb. "You're looking at him. Got the idea out of a catalog for assemble-it-yourself furniture. Cheap *and* easy. I had them ship out enough for ten rooms. Only got one done because the construction crew walked off."

Showed their good taste.

"I know what they did—it's not that hard. It's like building blocks for adults. Stuff even comes with detailed instructions," Will enthused. "I'm going to find a high school kid to help me do the rest."

"No. Don't." She put her hand out like a traffic

cop. "See if you can return the unused materials."

"Why? I thought this was *genius*. People want their computers and need lots of outlets."

"This is an *historic* hotel. Guests will come here to experience the flavor of that era. It's one thing to provide modern amenities with Internet access, WiFi, and outlets. It's a completely different thing to destroy the very thing guests would flock to see."

He shook his head and looked around. "What am I supposed to do with this room?"

"I don't know." *If the local hospital was short on space, maybe he could rent it out as an isolation unit.* "I'll figure something out." She glanced at her watch. "I have to leave now, or I'll miss my appointment with Emma."

Will looked stricken. "So soon?"

"It's part of my job. I interview everyone." Her heart twisted with pity. "I have an idea."

His face brightened. "Yeah?"

"While I'm gone, you can get rid of those tire planters."

His face fell. "I made those."

They make the place look like a bunch of hillbillies live here.

Tallulah handed him a frowny face sticky note. "Perhaps there's another place you can put them to good use?" *Out of sight. Away from the hotel.*

Will pouted. "What am I supposed to do with the flowers?"

She put her fists on her hip. "Put the plants in the ground around the wraparound porch."

He needed *something* to keep him out of trouble.

His shoulders slumped. "All right."

"And while you're at it, think about a sign. Something wooden, not that ugly thing you can barely see from the road."

He opened his mouth, and she slapped another frowny face sticky note in his hand.

"And not neon. A painted wooden sign, with a light that shines on it so people can see it."

Will nodded like a little boy caught with his hand in the cookie jar.

"Go out and play in the dirt. It will do you good."

Will trudged out the door ahead of her.

"Well," Lucius whispered in her ear, "was I wrong?"

She jumped. "Stop sneaking up on me. No, you were right. This room is a nightmare."

A satisfied expression crossed his face.

"Don't get too smug," she warned. "I need to pull a jack rabbit out of a hat to fix this place."

"If anyone can do it, it's you. You're a powerful Medicine Woman, Tallulah. You just don't know it yet."

He vanished before she could retort that it would take *two* Medicine Women to fix the place.

Tallulah made sure Franny had lots of fresh water and was safely ensconced in her paw print bed in the hotel room before setting out for Little Big Horn Battlefield. No radio, no audio books, just blessed quiet reigned—now that Lucius wasn't whispering in her ear, jumping out of showers, or talking to her behind Will's back.

Flat, wide-open spaces and clouds that looked as if a great artist stroked the deep blue sky with a cotton tipped paintbrush met her gaze when she took her eyes off the asphalt. She was used to flat plains and wide expanses in Oklahoma, but here the color of the earth, the sky, the rolling hills, waving grass, and the clouds gave her the same sense of sacred grounds she'd experienced in the Pictograph Caves.

Relaxed and at peace, at last, she enjoyed the easy sixty-mile drive. After lunch, she intended to spend a few hours exploring the battlefield, but right now she had to find the restaurant.

Emma had told her the trading post sat right across from the main entrance to the national monument visitor center. Hard to miss really, given the huge arrow pointing at the entrance. Teepees sat in front of the restaurant, mute testimony to an old way of life. The building, draped in red, white, and blue bunting, bore stars, antlers, and skulls of cattle, a Wild West blend of animal trophies and patriotic profusion. She was to meet Emma at the restaurant, but she didn't specify where. Pots of flowers exploding with red, white, and purple blooms lined the walkway. Tallulah walked the length of the extensive wooden porch and decided to go into the store to look for her.

A riot of colors, sounds, and smells overwhelmed Tallulah when she stepped inside. Glass cabinets and counters showcased collectible and expensive artwork. Displays of Native American textiles, souvenirs, books, puzzles, and toys vied for her attention as she wandered the aisles. She stopped in front of a large stone fireplace decorated with the enormous head of a buffalo and searched for Emma's long black braids and quick smile. The smell of fry bread wafted by, and her stomach growled.

"Hello!" Emma called from the one side of the

store she hadn't searched.

"Thanks for meeting me. What a place. I don't know where to look first. I'm in sensory overload."

"Ha! Wait until you bite into an Indian taco. Then your taste buds will be singing and dancing too."

They chose a table inside the restaurant. As promised, the taco was divine, the service was friendly, and the price was right. Between bites of food, Tallulah encouraged Emma to tell her about her time at the Hotel LaBelle. She wanted to get to know her better. She couldn't put her finger on it, but something told her Emma was more than just a maid.

"Will's got a gambling problem. Lost a lot of money at the casino and owes more than he's making."

"Wait," Tallulah put her fork down. "I thought he played the ponies?"

"That too." Emma sipped her soda. "He's up to his eyeballs in debt, owes me a month's pay, and the contractors walked off because he fell behind paying them too."

Tallulah looked Emma in the eye. "You're working for free? Why do you stay?"

"Let's just say, I have a vested interest in the place, especially now that he's gotten it halfway back on track." She threw her hands up. "But, I can't help feeling something's off about Will. Not just the gambling thing. The guy shows up out of nowhere with a pile of money and says he wants to invest in a ruin of a hotel."

"Pile of money? As in cash?" Tallulah pulled out her large pad of sticky notes and black marker. "How much?"

"He says three hundred thousand." Emma bit on

her taco and moaned. "Delicious."

"The bank must have wondered where it came from. There are regulations about how much cash you can carry around. Laws put in effect to keep drug lords and terrorists from laundering money."

Emma nodded. "He said he had a bill of sale from a property in California, but it sounded fishy to me all the same."

Tallulah wrote, *Follow the money.*

"Some of my friends on the rez tell me he's in deep Buffalo dung with some bad guys." Emma shook her head. "They play for keeps."

"Making him even more anxious to get the hotel back up and running." Tallulah wrote, *Desperate.* "Bad combination. Broke, in deep debt, and desperate."

"Exactly."

Emma tried to pay for lunch, but Tallulah slapped her cash down first. "This is on me."

"How about if I take you for a stroll around the battlefield? Walk off some of that fry bread? I've heard the rangers tell the stories so often, I can repeat them for you."

"I'll drive," Tallulah said.

As she pulled through the national monument entrance, a pall of silence fell upon the two women. Without saying a word, Emma climbed out of the SUV and led Tallulah through the visitors' center, bypassing the souvenirs and history books. They stood outside in the shade of a green overhang, surveying the expanse of grass, rolling hills, and tombstones on a nearby ridge.

"This is where the ranger usually has the program. It's pretty good, with perspectives of both the Native Americans and the white men." She smiled. "One of the rangers always calls the white men illegal immigrants, which makes me laugh. I prefer the Crow Nation tour. You get the real deal with that one. Today, you get me—guess you could say I'm your personal Crow tour guide."

They stood together in silence, the weight of over a hundred and forty years of history and the deaths of white men and countless Native Americans pressing upon Tallulah. A battle won by the Native Americans, but the war won by the whites forcing the real landowners onto the reservations with a diet of rancid meat, fatty bacon, flour, and coffee. Death of the spirit by enslavement. Death of a culture by domination.

Dotted with white stone markers where the white men were buried where they fell, the rolling green hills held fewer red stone markers where oral history said Native Americans fell. Their bodies were quickly retrieved by their tribes and buried in trees, caves, or scaffolds. Overwhelmed by sadness, Tallulah closed her eyes.

An ear shattering explosion erupted overhead. A man screamed, "It's a good day to die!" Tallulah fell to the dirt and covered her ears, but the noise pulsed in her bones. The ground thundered. Men shouted, "More ammo! More ammo!" Guns roared. Smoke filled her lungs. Someone shrieked and fell with a thud in front of her, kicking gravel and dust into her face. Trembling like an aspen in a windstorm, Tallulah dared to peek through her fingers. A white man's head fell in front of her, his eyes wide, mouth still open in a scream, crimson blood splattering on her hands. Heart in her throat, she crab walked backward into a wall and lay facedown, hands over her head, shuddering and sobbing, until someone grasped her shoulder and rolled her over.

"Tallulah, can you hear me?"

"Emma?" she whispered. "You're okay? Where did the bomb come from?"

She shook her head. "There was no bomb."

Tallulah sat up and leaned against the wall, her heart drumming an erratic beat. A crowd of people encircled her, staring at her and talking to each other, concern and fear playing across their faces, voices rising and falling in waves. Someone recommended calling the park rangers.

Emma turned and faced the crowd. "She's okay. You can go on your way."

"There was an explosion." Tallulah held her hands up. "Blood. There was blood on my hands."

Nothing. Not a drop of red.

"I heard guns, men screaming—it was a war zone."

"It's just not fair." Emma pulled Tallulah to her feet. "I've been to a sweat lodge and even spent a week fasting in isolation on spirit quests. Nothing. *You* show up on a beautiful day, sit down in a nice restaurant, have a delicious Indian taco, and what happens? You have a vision. Not just any vision. No, *you* see the Battle of Little Bighorn."

Shaking and disoriented, Tallulah repeated, "It felt so real. Like the man in the cave, only worse, much worse."

"You see visions." Emma grabbed her upper arms and stared directly into her eyes. "Tell me the truth. Have you been seeing Lucius Stewart?"

Chapter Four

Lucius sat on a rocker on the porch and watched the clouds pile into a quilt of blue, purple, red, and orange overhead. Even after more than a century, he never tired of the spectacular Montana sunset, and he yearned to share his gratitude for the Lord's simple gifts with another human being. The only living soul, other than animals, who knew he existed was off at the Crow Reservation. As if taking land away from the original owners and forcing them into an area a tenth of what used to be rightfully theirs could be "reserved."

The thought of Tallulah visiting his old stomping grounds filled him with nostalgia. Many a fine day and night had he spent among the Crow people—although they sure hadn't been over the moon with him in the beginning. Over the course of time, he worked hard to earn their trust, to prove he wasn't another lying white man trying to steal from them. He thought he won everyone over—until the night Beautiful Blackfeather cursed him. Unbidden, his thoughts strayed back to the first day he and Mourning Dove actually spoke.

That morning, Lucius had been heading to the brand new post office in downtown Billings. Two cowpokes staggered up to a beautiful, young Crow woman astride her horse. One man in a ratty cowboy hat, filthy denim trousers, and mud encrusted boots planted himself in front of her blue roan and grabbed at the rein. "Wall, I'll be. Here's a purdy Injun gal."

Another man with a sweat-darkened bandana hanging loose around his throat, and a cigarette hanging out of the corner of his mouth, grabbed at the woman's leg and missed, slapping the roan's flank. He raised a bottle, waved it in her direction, and leered at her. "Bet she'd like some fire water."

The woman yanked back at the reins, and the horse danced to one side, then the other, but the cow punchers had her hemmed in.

Predators. He'd seen enough of their kind on the streets of New York City and had tossed plenty of drunks out of the bars of hotels where he'd worked. They always underestimated him. "Hey there fellas, you look like you been up all night celebrating. Ain't it time you got some rest?" He preferred trading words to trading punches. After all, they might be his customers someday. Unlikely, but one never knew.

The one with the smoke turned and glared at him with his one good eye, the other hidden behind a black eye patch. "Mind your own business, ya mail order cowboy."

Lucius examined his coat sleeves as if he'd never seen them before. "Ah, I could see why you might think that I'm just a tenderfoot out for a short spell to see the sights. But as you can tell from Old Betsy"—he opened his jacket and exposed his Colt Six Shooter—"I've been here quite a while. I own a lovely place of lodging on the edge of town. Perhaps you've heard of the Hotel LaBelle?"

The drunkards glanced at each other and shook their heads.

"No? It is a delightful establishment. I have the

softest beds in town, the finest wine, and a piano player so skilled he puts the birds to shame. You really must stop in sometime."

"We don't want nothin' to do with your fancy pants bed-house. Mind your own business, and we'll get along just fine."

"Oh, but this lovely woman is my business." He stepped up to the horse and grabbed her hand. She favored him with a stoic look but didn't resist. "You see, we're courting. She and I have been seeing each other for some time now."

Not a lie. In fact, he'd seen her selling her exquisitely beaded bags and moccasins to the owner of Lamont General Store on the first day he arrived in town in 1900. The shopkeepers bought her handwork for pennies, and then sold them for dollars to sightseers and souvenir seekers. Pretending interest in purchasing a bag for a female relative back east, Lucius chatted up the storekeeper and learned the girl's name was Mourning Dove. The granddaughter of an Indian scout for the ill-fated men led by General George Armstrong Custer, she traveled sixty miles each month from the reservation to bring her work to the store and to buy supplies. Only the bitter winds and deep winter snows kept her away.

Lucius made a habit of trying to be in the shop when he saw her coming. Over the course of two years, they exchanged no words but many side glances. At times, he imagined a flicker of interest in her eyes but brushed the thought off. What would a beautiful young woman like her want with an old man like him?

"If she ain't no strumpet," One-Eye sneered, "then why don't she have no ring on her finger?"

Lucius shook his head and wagged his finger at the man. "Now you've gone and ruined my surprise. I was on my way to the new post office hoping to secure that very thing. Placed my order weeks ago, but you know what the mail's like."

Mourning Dove squeezed his hand and then sign talked, "You fill my heart with joy."

Oh, she was a quick one.

"Now, if you boys don't mind, I need some private time with my fiancée. I'm sure there's some painted ladies pining away for you back in the saloon."

"C'mon," One-Eye plucked at the other cowpoke's sleeve. "Let's go see if that there redhead and her friend is ready to have some more fun."

After the wranglers staggered back into the saloon, Lucius allowed a huge sigh of relief and shaky laughter to escape. When he stepped aside to allow Mourning Dove to be on her way, instead, she slid off the horse, threw her arms around him, and kissed him. Since then, he'd never wanted another woman. Until now.

In many ways, Tallulah reminded him of Mourning Dove. Smart, independent, hardworking, and stubborn, the blonde with the wild hair could have been the brunette with the long black braid's spirit sister. He shivered at the idea of the two of them together. Without a doubt, they'd gang up on him and have him wrapped around their little fingers. Tallulah, with her modern ways was as foreign to him as Mourning Dove had been in the beginning. But he learned about the Crow Nation and more.

Over the century, he had been a fly on the wall, watching and listening to every human that found his or her way to the hotel. He'd learned a lot about drugs from watching the teenagers who'd smoked what he thought was tobacco at first. After seeing how they behaved, he realized they weren't smoking peace pipes. The workmen carried boxes of music that blasted eight hours a day, a lot of wailing about pickup trucks, bad times, whiskey, and broken hearts.

The big black things with screaming heads, those TVs, they scared him. Not because he thought they were supernatural. No, they frightened him because they spoke about wars, bombs, and hate. Even Will would shake his head and say, "Why don't we ever hear any good news?" At those times, Lucius was grateful to be sentenced to the hotel, a haven of safety, away from the violence on the other side of the porch railings. He could learn about Tallulah's world too, he just hoped it wasn't what he saw on those screens.

Where in blue blazes had that dang woman gotten to, anyway? She planned to go for lunch and come back, these days that meant an afternoon trip at best. She'd been gone close to the entire day. Out alone on the roads, she could get lost. Never make it back. After a century of contributing both sides of every conversation, if something happened to Tallulah, what would he do? Who would he talk to? Just as the sun hit the horizon and extinguished itself, frantic barking erupted from inside the hotel.

Something was wrong with Franny!

In two shakes of a tail feather, he materialized in Tallulah's room.

Hysterical yapping came from behind the closed bathroom door, and Will Wellington, that swindler, rummaged in the nightstand.

Lucius yelled and grabbed the man's shoulders,

"What are you doing in here, you scoundrel?"

Will paused for a moment, shook his head, and slammed the drawer shut. He swore a blue streak and shoved his hand under the mattress, running it the length of the bed. Failing to find anything, he cast wild looks around the room. He strode to the dresser, yanked out a drawer, and patted the underwear stacked neatly within. Slamming that shut, he pulled Tallulah's suitcase off the shelf and searched the outside and inside pockets. Will yanked the bathroom door open.

Panting, tongue lolling, Franny bolted out of the space and barreled into Lucius' feet. Yipping with joy, she pawed at his legs until he reached down and rubbed her soft ears.

"There, there, it's okay, little girl, I won't let him hurt you."

He glanced up and saw Will's gaze riveted on the little pug. A moment later, he tossed the suitcase back up on the shelf and fled the room, slamming the door behind him.

Lucius slid down to the floor, welcomed Franny onto his lap, and patted her until she began to snore.

Where was Tallulah?

****

"Lucius Stewart appeared in my room the first night I arrived at the hotel."

Tallulah sipped a cup of coffee and tapped the table. The crowd of horrified onlookers at the site had dissipated, thank God, leaving her alone with Emma and her own embarrassment. Still shaking, Tallulah asked Emma to go back to the trading post with her to give her a chance to recover from her vision. She'd never experienced one quite like that before and didn't feel up to driving back to Billings yet.

Emma waved a waitress over for a refill on both coffees. "Was he angry?"

"Oh, no. Shocked I could see him, though. In fact, totally amazed might describe his reaction better. He asked me all sorts of thoughtful questions, like he'd been dying to talk to someone—anyone—for an eternity. Which, I guess is true." She took a sip of the brew. "He hates Will Wellington, keeps calling him a thief."

"So, he's not just like a moving picture, where you can see him but he isn't aware of you?"

"He's highly aware of and interacts with me. Although there were times this morning I wanted a little less interaction." She laughed. "He danced around the kitchen talking to me while I interviewed Will. *I* could see him—oh, and Franny sees him. But Will doesn't."

A thoughtful look crossed Emma's face. "Do you think he's attractive?"

"Will? Yuck. No." Tallulah shuddered.

"I meant Lucius."

A warm flush crept up her neck. "If he were a living, breathing guy, seriously, what's not to like? Tall, dark, those shoulders, and jeez, those eyes, well a girl can get lost in them. He has a wicked sense of humor, dimples that make me think he's teasing me all the time, and a voice that makes my legs weak..." The spectacular Big Sky sunset made her wish she was sitting on the Hotel LaBelle porch, sipping wine, and laughing with that very man—ghost, whatever he was.

Emma gave her a hard stare.

Embarrassed, Tallulah gave a little laugh. "Wow. I don't sound desperate much, do I?" She put her hands over her face. "I have the hots for a dead man. Lord, I must be crazy."

"You're Choctaw, you say?" Emma drew a circle in the coffee drippings on the table. "How much?"

"Oh, I'm guessing a quarter, at least. My grandmother raised me after my parents died in a car crash."

"And she was a Medicine Woman?"

Tallulah nodded, remembering her grandmother and her powerful personality. A tiny dynamo, Grandmother never let her get away with anything, despite the fact that her granddaughter towered over her by fifth grade.

"What about your mother? Did she have visions too?"

Tallulah nodded, and hot tears spilled down her cheeks. "This trip has triggered all sorts of visions—you saw what happened today." She lowered her voice. "I'm afraid I'm turning into my mother."

"Why? What happened?" Emma leaned in. "Tell me everything."

"After she had me, she began to have visions. My grandmother told her it was okay, part of her heritage. And not to tell anyone outside the family." Tallulah lifted the cup with a trembling hand. "One day, when she was at the grocery store one town over, she saw a man attack a woman with a knife. She screamed for help. The police came—and took my mother to the psychiatric hospital."

Emma frowned. "There was no attack?"

"Not at that point in time. She saw an incident that had occurred ten years before, a cashier was attacked and murdered by her ex-husband. The police and the manager knew the story, but my mother wasn't familiar with the store. She had no idea."

Emma blew out a long breath. "Let me guess, they thought she was hallucinating."

Tallulah nodded. "The doctors sent her home on enough medications to fell a horse. I was still a baby, so I don't recall anything. My grandmother said she was like a zombie, shuffling around in a daze. Then one day, she snapped out of it and was her old self."

"Good news?"

"Yes and no. She threw her medications out—and was fine for a while."

The waitress came by and placed the check on the table.

"Until?"

"My father and mother went on a trip together. He thought it would be good for her to get out of town, just the two of them. He took her to Longhorn Mountain."

Emma's eyes widened. "What was he thinking? That's one of the most sacred sites in Oklahoma. Even now, people go there for spirit quests and to pray."

"My grandmother said he was a nice German man from a Lutheran farm family and didn't believe in ghosts or spirits." Tallulah shook her head. "I think he may have been like a parent trying to prove to a child there's no boogeyman under the bed. Except in this case, there was. My grandmother thinks she had a vision while they were driving—they were going around a bend and the car went off the road."

The waitress returned and said, "Ladies, sorry to do this, but we're closing now."

"We overstayed our welcome." Tallulah placed a ten on the table. "Keep the change."

A few moments later, Emma and Tallulah stood outside in the parking lot shivering in the suddenly cool air.

Emma yanked open the door to her pickup. "What plans do you have for tomorrow?"

"Having a come-to-Tallulah talk with Will first thing in the morning."

"I'd like you to meet some people tomorrow. Can you do that?"

"Well, technically, I'm on Will's clock. He's paying for my time."

Emma snorted. "He's behind paying everyone else. What makes you think he's going to pay your bill?"

"Now that you put it that way…"

"Dinner at five, my place." She scribbled an address and phone number on a scrap of paper. "Some of my family members are in from out of town. I'd like you to meet them."

As Tallulah waved goodbye to Emma, she wondered what she should wear. She'd go through her closet, see what looked presentable. Maybe Lucius could help her pick something out.

Oh my God. I'm thinking about asking a ghost for fashion advice. I must be losing my mind.

Chapter Five

When Tallulah's car appeared, a wave of relief rolled through Lucius. He must have paced ten miles on the wraparound porch while waiting for her. She stepped in front of her car, backlit by the headlights.

Damn, she has a fine figure.

In his mind, he couldn't help comparing Tallulah's curves to those women who showed up last spring. When the snowmelt ran off the mountains, two boxy vehicles had turned up and disgorged a small army of skinny females and a few men with bulky equipment. Giggling and chattering about a "shoot" for Veronica and her secrets while Will drooled over their credit cards, they registered and filled all twenty rooms of the hotel, even the barely livable ones.

Early the next morning, Lucius watched in astonishment as the models, clad only in one or two tiny swatches of cloth, waded into the shallow river while the photographer kept hollering, "Try to look like you're having *fun!*" The water had to be freezing and those gals may as well have been naked. They all looked like they needed a good meal, or three.

Tallulah on the other hand, not only relished her food, but wore it well, with curves in all the right places. These new fashions showed off her voluptuous shape. Denim had *never* looked that good in his time.

"Will, is that you?" Her husky voice carried across

the summer breeze just as the headlights went out.

Lucius snorted. "I can't believe you mistook me for that weasel. He took off hours ago like the Devil was chasing him."

Stepping onto the dimly lit porch, Tallulah favored him with a great big grin.

Was that his heart thumping like a drum during a sun dance?

He could go for a year on that smile, maybe longer. Even in this light he could see her eyes sparkle. She seemed happy to see him.

Or was he just fooling himself?

"Ah, the very man I wanted to talk to—right after I get Franny and take her out for a walk. She must think I abandoned her."

Heart leading his hand, he touched her arm as she went to pass by.

She stopped, turned, and stared. "Lucius. Your hand."

He stared at his tingling fingers and dropped his hand. "I'm sorry, I shouldn't have done that."

"No, that's not what I meant." She shook her head. "I felt you. *Really* felt your touch. How is that possible?"

He touched his chin. "Lord have mercy, Tallulah, I can feel my face."

She placed her fingertips on his cheek as gently as if she was catching a butterfly. A century of longing to be seen and touched shuddered and shimmied through him. He turned his face and kissed her palm, allowing himself the pleasure of lingering, basking in her warmth and the amazement that he felt her, really felt her.

She gasped. "Oh my God, what's happening?"

He placed her hand on his chest. "I don't know, but my heart's bucking like a bronco, and I can't stop thinking about—"

Headlights bounced up and down the dirt road and a horn honked.

Lucius peered into the darkness. "What the heck?"

"Must be Will. I'm going inside, getting Franny. We'll talk later."

"I gotta tell you something about that lizard—"

"Later," she yelled over her shoulder.

Ear glued to his itty-bitty phone, Will stomped up the stairs and walked within inches of Lucius. Curious, he followed the swindler who raced behind the registration desk and into his office.

What flew up his nose?

Lucius slid behind the counter and watched from the door.

Will jerked books from the shelves, flipped through the pages, and threw them to the floor one after another. Next he ransacked the desk, the very one where Lucius had spent many a happy hour. Drawers flew open under his frantic fingers with curses Lucius didn't know were legal in Montana.

"C'mon, c'mon, I know yer here somewhere," Will slurred. "Yer holding out on me, I know it. The gold's gotta be somewhere. Stewart was loaded."

Lucius suppressed a groan. *The drunken idiot thought he was on a treasure hunt.* There was no gold hidden here. Lucas took every penny he had to the bank to pay off the loan on the hotel. With all the construction, if there had been a dime left, Will would have found it by now. After all this time, why was he acting like a lunatic *now*?

Will walked across the room, and the floor creaked.

"That's it!" Will raced out of the office and ran right through Lucius.

Doubled over, Lucius dry heaved and white-knuckled the doorjamb.

What's happening to me?

He glanced up in time to see Tallulah trot past the desk, Franny at the lead in a whirl of panting, barking, and snorting. The screen door slammed behind the pug and her owner. Will stomped back into the office, a crowbar in his hand.

Lucius stepped aside, taking care to stay out of his way.

Will knelt down, flipped the area rug back, and began to pry at a board.

"You son of a gun, you're destroying the place!"

Deaf to Lucius' warning, Will ripped at the hardwood and pulled a chunk back. Cuss words poured out of his mouth.

He had to warn Tallulah. *The man was drunk and crazy.* Lucius blinked. When he opened his eyes, he was in her room. *Dammit. Wrong place.* He focused on the porch—

****

"Franny, slow down, I'm going to break an ankle in a rabbit burrow." Tallulah pulled back on the leash, nearly lifting the harness-wearing pug in the air. "You won't catch anything out here tonight except a chill."

Panting and snuffling, the little dog scrutinized each blade of grass, searching for exactly the right spot to do her duty. At last she found the perfect place.

"About time, Princess Franny." Tallulah rubbed

her sweater-clad arm, regretting leaving her heavier jacket in the room. She'd been in such a rush to get her dog outdoors, she hadn't even had a moment to reflect on the strange occurrence with Lucius. Strange wasn't the right word. *Disturbing? Unsettling? Exciting? Thrilling? Arousing?*

Tonight's turn of events had been more than a little odd. First of all, he was ghost, a spirit, a vision. Not tangible. But now, the memory of touching him, the softness of his kiss in her palm, set off waves of pleasure in her core. She shook her head.

This was nuts. No sane woman would be having fantasies of a ghost next to her on that big four poster, running his fingers through her hair, pressing his lips against hers, and tracing her face with his fingertips. But, oh, the prospect of loving him all over was one she couldn't stop thinking about. One touch, one tender kiss told her he'd be a gentle lover.

She shook her head. In some ways she wasn't that different from Lucius. She lived on her own, rarely went out socially, and had all her food delivered to avoid crowds. Come to think of it, *she* might be more of a hermit than he was. He welcomed company. Her? Not so much—until this trip. And now the only company she longed for was his. Geez. She really did need to get out more.

"Tallulah!"

Lucius' voice broke through her hormone-laced thoughts.

He stood on the walk in front of the porch steps, frantically waving his arms. "Get back here, now. It's important."

Franny yelped in surprise as Tallulah lifted her and

began running toward the hotel. What was he doing that far away from the building? How was that possible? Her left foot snagged on something, and she put her hands out to break her fall. The pug flew out of her arms.

"Franny!" She scrabbled to her feet, only to fall down again in pain-induced vertigo. "Franny," she sobbed. "Oh, my baby, I'm so sorry. Where are you?" She crawled forward on her hands and knees, crying tears of pain and fear, searching for her best friend, her companion, her little dog.

Halfway across the dirt driveway, a pair of boots came into her line of vision.

"Oh, Will, I'm hurt, and I can't find my dog. Can you help me, please?"

"Ya know, I'm beginning to get a little annoyed that you keep mistaking me for that horse thief."

She rolled over on her back and looked up at the most beautiful sight in the world.

Lucius Stewart held her panting pug in his arms, and she didn't look the least bit harmed for the fall. He squatted next to her and placed Franny on the ground. "See if you can get up on your good foot and lean on me."

Gingerly at first, then with more pressure, she wrapped her left fingers over his shoulder and hopped on her right foot across the driveway to the stairs. With one hand on Lucius and the other on the railing, she was able to make her way up the steps, the huffing and puffing pug hopping up behind her. She opened the screen door and limped inside, Lucius with her.

Glass broke and curses exploded from Will's office.

"Keep moving," Lucius spoke in a low voice. "He's in his cups. Take the elevator."

"I didn't know it worked," she whispered. "I've been taking the stairs all this time. Oh, well, good exercise."

He nodded and waited for her to open the ornate brass gate. "Just press the button. It only goes up or down."

At last they arrived at her door, and Franny pawed at the wood, urging her on. "Okay, I got it."

"You've got one more thing you gotta do before you get in that bed and put your foot up."

Sweat trickled into her eyes, and she wiped her brow. She was panting as hard as the pug. "What?"

He pointed toward the desk. "Put that chair under your doorknob and push it in tight-like."

After following his instructions, including putting two pillows under her foot, she collapsed on the bed. "I wish you could get some ice for my ankle."

"Before tonight, I couldn't even leave the porch." He sat on the bed next to her and locked gazes with her. "I have no idea what I can and can't do, anymore. All I know is, when I'm with you, I'm a changed man. I'm almost real."

She grabbed his warm, solid hand and squeezed. "You've always been real to me." The pug yapped, and she laughed. "And to Franny."

Lucius stroked her cheek with a light, easy touch. "You're the first woman I've wanted to be with in over a century, Tallulah. That has to be connected with this change coming over me. What other explanation can there be?"

She moved her leg and set off throbbing in her

ankle. "Oh, I don't know," she said through gritted teeth. "Full moon? Alignment of the planets? Magnetic fields?"

He leaned in close, and a heady blend of cigar, whiskey, and *real* man hormones wafted over her. Her gaze strayed to his cheek. The damn dimple sat there teasing her, urging her to come closer. She lifted up her chin and licked her lips.

"May I be so bold as to ask for a kiss from your lovely lips, Miss Tallulah?"

"Omigod, you're killing me." She laughed. "Kiss me, Lucius. Let's see if a kiss will undo your curse."

Their lips joined, not with a lightning bolt, but with a definite sizzle, one that took her breath away. His tongue probed her lips. *A good thing I'm laying down already or I'd be swooning.*

She opened her mouth to invite him in for a deeper connection—

Someone pounded on the door. "Ms. Thompson, I need to shee you righth now."

Where was Lucius? One moment he was kissing her, the next poof!

"I'm indisposed, Mr. Wellington." *And you have terrible timing.* "I'll see you in the morning."

The knob rattled, and the deadbolt shook. "Now. I need to shee you now."

"And I said no. If you don't go away, I will call the police."

He guffawed and rattled the knob. "No copsh out here. Jusht the Sheriff."

"You sound like you've been drinking. Go to bed. Sleep it off. We'll talk tomorrow."

"Yer making me very—"

The entire building shook and rattled.

Earthquake? Were there such things in Montana?

"Will?"

No answer. She raised herself up on her elbow and stared at the door.

"Lucius?"

Brushing his hands together, he appeared at the side of her bed, looking like the cat that ate the canary. "That lout won't be bothering us again tonight."

"Is he—"

"Dead? Heavens, no. But he *will* be aching in the morning."

"What did you do?"

"Let's just say I pulled the rug out from under him." He grinned and plopped down next to her on the big four poster, stretching his long legs and arms. "And he just *happened* to take a tumble down the stairs. He'll think he tripped and fell while drunk. Which he is."

She gasped. "That's awful. What if he's hurt?"

"Nah, he's fine. Drunks topple over all the time. They get bruised, might break a bone or something. The worst he'll have tomorrow is a bad hangover." He cleared his throat. "Look, I've been trying to tell you all evening, that swindler searched your room today. He even looked in your drawer of unmentionables."

"What a jerk." She knew he was a boor but had never pegged him for a pervert.

He quirked an eyebrow. "Are you calling him dried meat?"

She laughed. "I guess I am. But, seriously, what on earth could he have been looking for?"

"If I were a betting man, and I'm not, I'd say money." He described the scene in the office. "I think he might have gone to the casino to try to win some cash, lost it instead, and got boozed up. Now he's chasing El Dorado, and is he gonna be disappointed. I took all my money to the bank to pay off my loan and get my deed to the hotel the very same day Beautiful Blackfeather cursed me. He won't find a penny, much less a gold coin."

"He's *broke*." She covered her face and groaned. "I'll *never* get paid the rest of my fee now."

"Did you *really* think he was going to pay you?"

She peeked between her fingers. "Yes. He gave me a thousand-dollar deposit. Emma said the same thing. I should have never taken this consultation."

"But if you hadn't come here, then we would have never met."

Tallulah lowered her hands and rolled over, face to face with this man candy from a bygone era, when men were men and women were glad of it. "That's true. Whatever you are, ghost, spirit, vision, I do like you Mr. Lucius Stewart."

"I like you too, Miss Tallulah Thompson." He snuggled closer. "Now about that kiss."

Just like her fantasy, Lucius was in her bed, cuddling with her. His kisses were like butterscotch candies; she couldn't have just one. She pulled him closer with each touch of his lips and ran her fingers through his silky hair. Was this a dream or had he been real all along?

His attention moved from her lips to her neck, down to the hot-button spot on her shoulder. She slipped her hands under his shirt and stroked his chest. Hair, not a gorilla suit but a real man's hair, unwaxed, unshaven, unmodern, met her fingers. He was one hundred percent male, and she wanted to find out how far that manliness extended. She tugged at his shirt to pull it out of his pants.

He froze.

"What's wrong?" She leaned back and looked at his face. "Don't you want me?"

Jumping a ghost's bones hadn't been on her bucket list, but it was now. This hot specter was calling her to dance the horizontal mambo. What was wrong with her? She had never been one to leap into bed with a man the first week she met him. It was as if he'd crawled under her skin and used his gentle old soul to patch and fill the voids in her younger soul—and she wanted more.

"My darlin', I'm not sure what I want." He rolled over and sat on the edge of the bed with his back to her. "In my day, a woman who behaved like this was called a lot of different names, starting with brazen hussy and going on to worse ones."

Face burning with shame, angry words spilled out of her mouth. "Oh. Now you're going to get all moral on me? For Heaven's sake, man, you've been out of touch for over a century. Trust me, a *lot* has changed. And it's not just cars, computers, and telephones. Women won the right to vote. We aren't chattel anymore. We work outside the home and have careers. Or we work at home and have children and a family. We can even do both."

He stood and faced her, buttoning his shirt, saying not a word.

Suddenly he's the strong, silent type after hours of nonstop chatter. His unspoken contempt set her off again.

"We get to *choose* who we want to go to bed with and when, Lucius. Maybe it's too much for you to grasp, perhaps the curse and isolation made you a deeper shade of whatever color of stuck-in-the-mud you already were in a frontier town. I hear you were called 'Love 'em and Leave 'em Lucius.' Do me a favor, Lucius. Just leave, and don't even *pretend* you give a fig about me."

Gazing at her with sad eyes, Lucius' usual warm, mischievous smile was gone, wiped off his handsome face. He nodded, said not a word, and vanished.

Hot tears leaked down the side of her face, and sobs wrenched their way out of her. *Maybe I need to see a psychiatrist to get some of that zombifying medicine, so I won't feel this pain.* Even though they both wanted the same thing, to restore the beautiful Hotel LaBelle to her glory, what made her think this supernatural relationship could ever be real? A man trapped in a time warp like a fly in amber would never, ever think of her as an equal.

Chapter Six

Lucius paced the porch all night long, mentally kicking himself for messing things up with Tallulah. What was wrong with him? A smart, beautiful woman wanted to bed him and he hightailed it out of her room as if Old Scratch had been after him. Maybe the Devil *was* behind it. After all, hadn't every woman he'd ever cared for left him?

Firstly, his mother left him. Well, she didn't want to leave him, he knew that. She died of pneumonia, what some people called "the old man's friend." But she wasn't a man, and she wasn't that old. He was thirty when she passed on, and his mother a healthy fifty. She worked herself to the bone for those rich, snot-nosed brats. A seamstress by trade, she'd made exquisite gowns for the high and mighty of New York society. Smart, funny, creative, and stubborn, his mother would never let a competitor take on any of her clients, lest they leave her. Well, she left them. In a pine box. Caught in a downpour after delivering her last creation, a wedding cake of a dress, his mother came down with a cough that wouldn't let up. The doctor came, shook his head, and urged her to get her affairs in order. Two weeks later, she died.

Then, all the lonely widows and divorcees on their adventures out to the Wild West came through Billings, took one look at his long fingers, and dragged him into bed. Not that he complained, mind you. He would be the first to acknowledge the services rendered had been his pleasure. The ladies never complained, but after a week of entertainment, they'd climb back on the train, smiling and satisfied, and leave. Billings was not San Francisco. There was no gold in the streets, therefore, no gold diggers stayed to keep his bed or his heart warm. Not that he wanted a woman who was only after his money, but it sure got lonely in the winter months when the trains rolled through town less often.

Finally, Mourning Dove. That woman drove him mad. Wouldn't live with him at Hotel LaBelle, wouldn't be seen with him in public—other than that one time with the cowpokes. Made him sneak out of town to a teepee halfway to the reservation, one she stayed in on trips into town to sell her wares. Didn't he send her samples back East to his mother's former client whose husband owned the department store with the big red star? The New Yorkers went crazy for the Wild West designs, couldn't get enough of her mirror bags, moccasins, and whatnot. On the rare occasion when she permitted him to travel to her home, he saw the Crow women lined up outside their teepees producing hundreds of pieces a week, all under Mourning Dove's close supervision. Every penny earned went into the Crow Nation coffers.

When Lucius asked why she gave up all her money, she laughed at him, shook her head, and called him *Crazy White Man*. "I have food, water, teepee, family, friends. What more do I need?"

"What about me? Don't you want me?"

"Yes, but we aren't really married until you come live in *my* home."

When couples married in the Crow Nation, the husband gifted the bride's parents with a horse and moved into the wife's home. She owned the teepee and all the household belongings, while he owned his horse and his weapons. In contrast to the white man's world, women in the matrilineal Crow Nation were highly respected and independent. Following tradition, Lucius gifted Beautiful Blackfeather with a horse, but Mourning Dove staunchly refused to move into Hotel LaBelle. He admired her free spirit but hated that she wouldn't marry him, no matter how hard he begged. She'd left him too, not in a pine box, but above ground, wrapped in her best robes, on a scaffold. The night Beautiful Blackfeather showed up to curse him, he *knew*. The lacerations on her arms, her hair cut at the base of her skull, her anger. Mourning Dove had been her only daughter. Childbirth was dangerous for mother and infant and he was responsible for her pregnancy. He might as well have pulled out a gun and shot his lover and the baby.

Lucius sat on a rocker, put his elbows on his knees, and dropped his head into his hands, moisture pricking the back of his eyelids. The century hadn't blunted the knife's edge of grief. Drowning in sorrow, neither alive nor dead, he was unable to be with Mourning Dove. Now, for the first time in decades, he'd hadn't been alone. Someone could not only sense him, but see and speak with him. His loneliness and grief had been set aside, and he'd had a glimpse of what life might be if the curse was removed. On the one hand, the idea thrilled him. On the other hand, that scared the dickens out of him.

Hotel LaBelle was his home, his sanctuary. Would

release from limbo evict him from his beloved inn? And what about Tallulah? Did this friendship born from her Medicine Woman powers have any chance of blossoming into a romance? Tallulah was smart, and damn independent, just like his beloved Mourning Dove. Soon she'd be gone too. And he'd be left behind alone—again.

He lost track of time and was surprised to see the sun rise as if nothing terrible had happened the night before. Birds chirped and took flight, the breeze stirred the grasses, and a small herd of mule deer waded into the river for a morning drink. He couldn't stand watching the beauty of the day unfold before him. The wine cellar stuffed with the collection of dead animal trophies would be a fitting place for him today.

****

After a fitful night's sleep, Tallulah sat up on the edge of the four poster and gingerly placed her left foot on the floor. "So far, so good." She stood and hobbled to the bathroom. On a scale of one to ten, the pain was about a four. Bearable and with some aspirin, it might even come down to a three.

Franny ran in circles, anxious to get out for her morning constitutional.

"We are moving slowly this morning, my little one. Patience."

The pug cocked her head to one side and watched her owner dress and pack her suitcase.

"If I go downstairs, it's a one way trip. We are not staying here another night. I'm fed up with Will's lies and have had it with Lucius."

The dog wagged her tail at his name.

"Now don't go giving me those big, sad eyes. If I

didn't promise Emma I'd drive out to the reservation to meet her family, I'd be on the first road out of town." Tallulah packed her laptop in the outer pouch of her travel bag. "This is the worst consulting job we've ever had. Why did I let you talk me into this?"

Placing the skeleton key in her pocket, she used the wheeled bag to assist her with walking.

Franny trotted ahead of her, snorting and snuffling. "What kind of idiot gets on a plane, drives halfway out into the hinterlands, and doesn't get paid at least half upfront? Well, that would be me, wouldn't it? Lesson learned."

Her left ankle throbbing, she pressed the button to the elevator and rode down in silence, mentally berating herself the entire time. Suitcase in the back of the SUV, she planned to get breakfast on the way to the reservation. The thought of breaking bread with Will made her gag.

Franny moseyed around the grass and nosed at each blade. Every stick was fascinating to the pug, it seemed. Tallulah hobbled slowly behind Franny, and the dog decided to go around the corner of the porch and behind one of the plants Will had moved from the tire planters to the ground. At least she'd gotten him to do *one* good thing with the place.

Tires crunched on the gravel driveway. With Franny deeply engrossed in her examination of the flowers, Tallulah could only peek around the corner. A black SUV with a mud-smeared Nevada license plate expelled two no-necked, enormous men with shaved heads, muscle shirts, and tattooed arms—the size of her thighs. If they spoke, it must have been in sub-vocal grunts to one another because she couldn't hear a word.

They stomped up the steps, one after the other, their denim encased legs ending in metal-tipped cowboy boots.

No luggage, but that could still be in the car.

If these guys were coming to register at Hotel LaBelle, Tallulah was doubly glad she was leaving. They looked like trouble with a capital T and that rhymed with "Get out of this place ASAP."

"C'mon Franny, what is taking you so long this morning? Didn't you get your bran flakes?"

The dog favored her with a baleful look, circled three times, and squatted.

Finally.

Franny finished her business, kicked up dirt with her back feet, and sniffed for another spot to water. And another. And another.

Tallulah sighed. *Better than in the car.*

An engine roared and the black SUV took off in a cloud of dust.

"Well that was quick. Let's go, Franny. We're out of here." She patted her pocket for the car fob and found the skeleton key. "Oh shoot. I have to take this back in." She and Franny climbed the stairs, Tallulah with difficulty, the pug hopping like a rabbit up the steps with no problem. "Show off."

She limped into the foyer over to the registration desk and set the key down on the counter. Just as she turned to go, she heard someone moan.

"Help!" Will's cry came from the office.

That can't be good.

Reluctant to enter the inner sanctum, Tallulah hobbled around the counter and stopped mid-limp.

Eyes, nose, lips, and ears bleeding, Will lay on his

back on the floor, cradling his left hand.

"Ohmigod! What happened to you?"

His eyelids and lips were rising like biscuits, and he struggled to speak. "The vig. I couldn't pay the vig. They sent the tune up squad."

Vig? She had no idea what he was talking about.

"I'm calling the Sheriff."

"No cops! Please. Make it worse."

"Two thugs just beat the crap out of you and you don't want to call the cops? What's going on here?" This had to be related to Will's gambling debts. Had those guys been from the Crow casino? No, their heads were shaved and the tattoos looked like stuff she saw on cop shows involving gangs.

He waved his right hand. "Help. Up."

"I can't lift you; you're going to have to pull yourself up on the desk. If you can get into the chair, I can roll you into the kitchen, get some ice on your wounds."

He nodded and, with great effort and grunting, slowly rolled over. Using only his right hand to pull himself to his knees, he fell into the chair and wheezed.

Avoiding piles of books, papers, and jutting floorboards, Tallulah leaned on the chairback to give her ankle a rest and rolled him into the kitchen. Her pug trotted behind her, dragging the leash. She tore open the freezer, pulled out bags of frozen food, and began applying them to every wound she could see. He cradled his left hand with his right one and moaned.

"Show me your hand," she ordered.

A long straight gash across the back of his hand bled, and all five fingers went in odd angles.

"What did they do to you?"

"Smashed. In. Drawerrrr."

Her stomach roiled, and she was grateful it was empty.

"More ice and you need to go to the hospital. Your hand and fingers look broken."

"No. No hospital. No questions."

"Are you out of your mind? You could get an infection? Your fingers could be in the wrong place the rest of your life!" She poured crushed ice into a plastic bag and put a towel on his lap. "Put your hand on this." She tried to curl his fingers back into place.

He screamed, and she stopped.

"This is nuts, Will." Fists on her hips, she stood in front of the injured man and shook her head. "What are you going to do? Sit here in pain for the rest of the week?"

"Pills. Desk."

"Oh great, you want me to touch that mess? I'll look, but don't be surprised if I can't find them."

The office looked as if it had vomited paper, books, and wood everywhere. Grumbling as she threw papers to the floor to get to the surface of the antique desk and the small drawers, she jumped and gasped when someone tapped her on the shoulder.

"Tallulah," Lucius said, "I have to show you something."

"Stop sneaking up on me," she hissed. "I thought you were one of the thugs." She turned to face him. "Did you see what happened to Will?"

He shook his head.

"Pop into the kitchen, why don't you? He's a trainwreck." She continued to search for the pills. Just as she spotted a brown plastic container, Lucius popped back into the room. She shoved the bottle into her back pocket.

"Someone sure settled his hash." He shook his head. "Guess he owed money to a big toad."

"He said he couldn't pay the vig, whatever that is."

"Look," Lucius pointed at the side of the desk. "See that diamond pattern?"

Still angry at him for his holier-than-thou behavior the night before, she could barely look at him, much less admire the craftsmanship of the wooden inlays. "What about it?"

"Press on the top and bottom point of the third diamond down from the top."

"Why?"

"C'mon, just do this, please?"

Pushing on the spots he indicated, she felt the wood give way. She pulled at the edges and the diamond came completely out of the side of the desk, exposing a space.

"Reach in and poke around with your finger."

"So a spider can bite me?"

"No."

She slid her finger into the void and felt a piece of paper. Sliding it up with care, she unfolded the document and began to read out loud.

"The Cattleman's Bank and its representatives, having been paid in full for the mortgage and interest due, hereby release Lucius Stewart from all debt in relationship to the loan of the Hotel LaBelle and grants this deed of ownership of said property to Lucius Stewart, his heirs and assigns from this day forward..." She stopped reading. "It's the deed to the hotel."

"Keep it with you, please?" His face was so sad,

even his moustache drooped. "I'm afraid that fool is going to chop the desk up looking for gold he won't ever find."

"Not saying I'll keep it forever." Lacking a suitable bag or pocket, Tallulah slid the deed under her blouse. "I'll hang on to it until I figure out what to do with it. What with you being dead and all—"

"It's complicated." Lucius put his hands up in surrender. "I get the picture."

"Hey!" Will shouted from the kitchen. "My pills?"

"My master calls." Tallulah pulled the container out of her pocket and turned it over. "These aren't even his. They're for some guy named Thomas Wilson, from a pharmacy in Las Vegas."

"Must have stolen them."

"Wait." She closed her eyes and visualized the SUV. "The thugs had a Nevada license plate." She tapped her chin with her index finger. "Emma told me he showed up here with three hundred thousand in cash, claims he sold a property." She spun on her heel and teetered. "Damn ankle." Tallulah hobbled and cursed her way back to the kitchen. She flicked Will's broken hand with her index finger.

He yowled. "What the hell are you doing?"

"This medicine was prescribed for a Thomas Wilson. That's not your name. Or is it?"

Will struggled to an upright position and bags of frozen vegetables slid off his face. His bloodshot eyes glared at her with rage. "Hand 'em over."

"Swelling's better, I see." She stepped out of range of his grasp. "So your name is really Thomas Wilson? And you're from Vegas?"

He looked away. "Yeah."

"Where'd you get the money for this place? A loan shark?"

Will, aka Wilson, shook his head. "Sold a motel to a mobster. Was gonna build a casino."

"And the mobster is so happy with his purchase, he sends his guys out a year later to rearrange your face?" She threw the pill bottle at him. "You're a lying sack of manure. I'm out of here."

She pivoted and smacked into Lucius. He must have been standing behind her the whole time. Tallulah shook her head and walked around him into the lobby. "Franny? Where are you? We're leaving."

The pug sat up, yawned, and got to her feet in slow motion. When she spotted Lucius, she danced in circles and yapped at his feet. He leaned over, rubbed her little ears, and said, "Hope to see you again sometime soon, funny-looking little dog."

Tallulah picked up the leash, stared him in the eye, and said, "Trust me, you'll never see this dog or this brazen hussy again."

The stricken look on his face told her the arrow hit its mark. But instead of feeling a thrill of victory, her heart thumped out a mournful rhythm of defeat.

"Tallulah—"

Blurry eyed, she fled the Hotel LaBelle and its two disturbing owners.

Chapter Seven

With eight hours to kill before dinner, Tallulah decided to take a pet-friendly day-long tour promoted on a travel website. Distracted by the tour guide's amusing banter, she was able to set aside her unsettling thoughts about Will Wellington, Hotel LaBelle—and Lucius. As Tallulah headed to Emma's for dinner, she cranked her music up as loud as she and Franny could bear it to drown out the thoughts racing through her mind like a hamster on speed. Show tunes mixed with rhythm and blues provided a sound track to her sixty-mile drive back in the direction of the battlefield. One of her favorite songs came on, and she belted out the lyrics.

Franny yapped and howled along with her. Hardly harmonious but amusing and distracting. She passed trailers hauling horses and pickup trucks filled with dogs, boxes, long wooden poles, and colorful canvases. Dark-haired children with large brown eyes pointed, smiled, and waved at the pug in the passenger window. Franny was a hit everywhere she traveled—even with ghosts. *Dammit*. She had to stop thinking about Lucius. It was over and done. Or would be if there'd ever been anything to be over in the first place. Romancing a living man was hard enough, what made her think it would be any different with a dead one?

The woman's voice in the GPS directed her to

follow the road for half a mile and turn right. As she crested the hill, the sight of hundreds of teepees sprawling over the dry brown plains took her breath away. Trying to drive and sightsee at the same time, Tallulah watched as still more canvas-wrapped poles rose from the ground, as if divine fingers lifted them from the earth. RVs, horse trailers, and pickup trucks encircled the camping area, like settlers' wagons of old. Children and dogs ran between the teepees, laughing and shrieking. Women of all sizes and ages stood in knots—laughing and talking with wide gesturing hands, signing to each other and their children. Between watching the people, listening to the GPS, and looking at the multicolored flags flapping in the breeze, she caught a few signs—"pow-wow," "rodeo," and "Indian relay races."

Holy buffalo! How had she forgotten the posters and flyers in Billings advertising the Crow Fair and Rodeo? Emma said she had family coming in from out of town, but neglected to mention it was the largest gathering of the Abssaalooke Tribe in the country. Tallulah hoped Emma didn't expect her to meet every single member. Maybe just Emma's clansmen?

Careful to avoid pedestrians and dogs, she found a parking spot on a narrow side street near the address Emma gave her—she hoped. To be safe, she called her new friend.

"Hey, I'm here, just parking around the corner." Tallulah climbed out of the car and went around to the passenger door. Franny required an assist down to the street. Princess pug took care of business in record time, then trotted ahead of Tallulah as if she knew the way.

"You're just in time. I've got a big pot of bison chili, and the wheel bread is on the stove. For dessert we have Indian berry pudding, *baalappia*."

Tallulah's stomach growled. "I never got breakfast because—well, I'll tell you in a minute." She rounded the corner and spotted Emma standing at her door, waving. She waved back, clicked off, and then put her phone in her pocket. The sound of drums filled the air, resonated in her chest, and followed her down the street. Practice for the big show, she guessed.

Franny jumped on Emma and wiggled her tail. "Happy to see you too, little one." She stood up from petting the pug. "I hope she likes other dogs. We have a bunch." Their hostess waved them indoors, and three large, mixed breed dogs greeted them with wagging tails. The little one leaped and attempted to run in circles, only to tangle the leash in the forest of dog legs and paws.

"Okay if I let her loose? She's dying to play."

"No problem." Emma laughed. "Looks like she'll be bossing the big dogs around. I have a fenced in backyard. I'll put all the 'kids' out there to play while we eat."

A man with bronze skin, high cheekbones, and jet-black hair rolled over to her in a wheelchair and extended his hand. A large black-and-white feather stuck out of the pocket of his blue chambray shirt.

"*Itchik diiawakaam.*"

"I'm sorry," Tallulah said as she shook his hand. "I don't speak Crow. I barely understand Choctaw."

"He said, 'Good to see you.' " Emma's face glowed with pride. "This is my hero brother, Bert Blackfeather. He's in town for the pow-wow. He lives in Washington, DC and works for Homeland Security. He fought in the Gulf War, got injured, won a Purple Heart *and* a Silver Star."

Bert flapped a hand at his sister. "Yeah, yeah, I'm a regular Joseph Medicine Crow."

Emma poked him in the shoulder.

"Nice to see you too, Bert. You must have an interesting job," Tallulah said.

He quirked a black eyebrow at her. "You like desk work?"

She laughed. "Only if it's a registration desk in a hotel."

Emma pointed at a kitchen chair. "You sit and talk. I'll get the food on the table."

"So—" Bert wheeled his chair into place and sipped a glass of water. "—I hear you see spirits."

That was fast, Tallulah thought. "Right to the point, aren't you?"

"He's not big on small talk," Emma called from the stove. "Either you love it or hate it."

Tallulah nodded. "Yes, I do. Not always fun, as your sister will tell you. My 'gift,' if you will, is unpredictable, like an uncontrolled seizure disorder."

Earthenware bowls of steaming chili and an iron skillet landed on a tile of the rainbow-colored tablecloth. The scent of fresh bread made Tallulah's mouth water.

Emma sat down and bowed her head. "We thank the great Creator for the bounty of His earth and for our family and friends, particularly at this time of year."

"Amen and let's eat." Bert pounced on the bread, cursing when he burned his fingers.

His sister laughed. "Serves you right."

"Just wait till you find your name on a Homeland watch list as the 'Hot Wheel Bread Terrorist.' "

She threw a piece at his head, and he snatched it out of the air with ease.

Movement by the kitchen caught Tallulah's eye. "Emma, shouldn't we have another place at the table?"

Emma's brow creased into a frown. "It's just us for lunch."

Tallulah pointed. "There's an elderly woman standing right there, by the stove. She's smiling and nodding at us."

Her hosts turned around, stared at the kitchen, then at each other.

Her mouth went dry, and her heart trip-hammered. "Don't you see her?" Silence answered her question. "Oh, crap. Not another one."

"Take a deep breath," Bert said softly. "It's okay. Describe her to us."

"She's awfully old and beautiful. Long black hair woven in two braids. So many creases on her face, it makes me wonder what she's seen with those sad brown eyes." Tears welled up in Tallulah's eyes. "Her dress—I think it's buckskin—the design in elk teeth. Two black-and-white feathers are sticking out of her hair."

Emma grabbed her hand and squeezed. "You're doing great."

"She's showing me her arms. Marks all over them." Deep gashes made those scars. "She's holding her arms, making a swinging motion like she's rocking a baby."

"Keep going."

"Hand talking. Signing. Something about a

mistake? Wrong. Right a wrong?"

Bert probed, "Anything else?"

"She's pointing at a cabinet—the one next to the sofa—and telling me to look. She's picking at the air—picking something up?" Tallulah glanced at her hosts. "Does this mean anything to you?"

Bert nodded. "For someone who said this was like a seizure, you are completely in control."

"Not really. If you guys weren't here, keeping me grounded, talking me through this, I'd be a puddle of poo."

The elderly woman folded her hands, placed them on the side of her face, and tilted her head.

"She's signing sleep—going to sleep? Not sure if she's going to sleep or she's been asleep? Can't really tell."

The vision shimmered, and the woman's moccasin covered feet began to disappear.

"I think she's leaving." Tallulah yearned to run over to the woman and touch her, but her trembling legs gave her no hope of that happening.

Emma cleared her throat. "Thank her and tell her we will do as she asks."

Tallulah said thank you and nodded. Bit by bit, the elder faded and disappeared.

Heart still drumming an erratic beat, she took a deep shaky breath. "Who *was* that?"

Emma and Bert exchanged a quick glance.

Emma pointed at the bowl. "Eat first, ask questions after."

A flash of recognition hit her like an arrow. "Omigod. She's Beautiful Blackfeather, the Medicine Woman, isn't she?"

Bert nodded. "Our great-great-great-grandmother."

****

Lucius watched that swindler, Will, Wilson, whatever his name was, roll across the kitchen floor and wrench open the freezer with his good hand. He grabbed two bags of vegetables and replaced the melted ice with peas and carrots. Then he opened the refrigerator and popped open a beer. After struggling to get the childproof cap open on the pill bottle, Will put the top between his teeth and bit down. Spitting out the white plastic top, he swallowed an indeterminate number of pills and washed them down with the entire can of beer. One beer followed another, until he passed out snoring.

"Hope you have a clean pair of pants handy, my friend." He tapped Will's head. "You are going to have a tough time getting to the outhouse when that beer hits."

Disgusted, Lucius popped onto the porch, his favorite thinking place. He leaned against the wall and crossed his arms. Sunset was a bit grayer than the previous evening and thick, dark clouds covered the normally big blue sky.

"Storm rolling in," he called to the mule deer in the river. "You might want to take cover."

One cocked a long ear at him and shook his head, as if to say, "Crazy White Man."

Yes, he was crazy. Crazy for making Tallulah run away. He pushed at a rocking chair, hard, and it barely moved. The night before, he'd been able to yank an area rug out from under a drunk. Today, his fingers, wispy and translucent, could scarcely do a thing. Here he was, a man sentenced to an eternity in limbo. When he met a woman who made him feel *whole* again, what did he do? Cut and run. What kind of fool does that? A frightened one. A man who'd rather be a shadow of himself than take a risk on an unknown future.

Lightning streaked across the sky, and a thunder clap followed shortly afterward—still a distance away. He sat down on the rocker and watched the clouds roiling above, mirroring his dark, churning feelings of inadequacy and self-loathing. He wished Beautiful Blackfeather had killed him. She could have cut his head off and mounted it on a piece of wood, like the animal trophies in the wine cellar. Eyes staring forward forever, he wouldn't have to see or feel a thing. Instead, in this in-between state, he felt everything, including regrets.

If only he'd been able to convince Mourning Dove to move in with him, none of this would have happened. She would have had a doctor with her when the baby was born, one that would have made sure both she and the baby survived the ordeal. Instead, her stubborn refusal to accompany him to the hotel had set this chain of events in motion. Beautiful Blackfeather's self-mutilation gave mute testimony to the magnitude of the loss she suffered. Clearly, both mother and infant died in childbirth, leaving her without a daughter and grandchild, and him without a wife or an heir. Pretty ironic, since both the deed to the hotel and his will stipulated all his property was to go to his heirs upon his death.

A three-prong bolt exploded out of the sky and a crash shook the hotel. *Getting closer*. He hoped Tallulah was out of the path of the tempest, somewhere safe. She'd said she was going to visit Emma

Horserider. He wondered what the housekeeper would tell her about Will and Hotel LaBelle that she hadn't told her on the first trip. What more was there to say about the conniving cheat? What could anyone do about the mess the loser made of things? Tallulah was gone. Lucius was disintegrating. His life's work was in the hands of a despicable man. *Could things get any worse?*

At least he still had his beloved Hotel LaBelle to haunt. Seeking light, some form of warmth, and yes, a bit of amusement at Will's expense, he rose and popped back into the kitchen to see if the crook had wet himself yet.

Flipped on its side, the desk chair was empty. Bags of vegetables and empty cans of beer lay scattered throughout the kitchen. How had that scoundrel been able to get up, much less walk? Where the dickens was he?

Lucius popped from room to room, searching for the phony. The trashed office remained devoid of human life, and the lobby, other than a trail of peas and carrots appeared the same. The elevator had no rider, sleeping or otherwise. Tallulah's empty room smelled of rose perfume. One by one, he popped in and out of the twenty usable rooms. No sight of Will. Even if he died, he couldn't just disappear. Lucius had been on the porch and would have seen the man stumble by him if he went to drown his sorrows in the river.

The basement? He found Will furiously twisting a large knob, his bad hand doing little to assist his good one. A sign on an adjacent copper pipe read, "Sprinkler system. Do not disable."

What was he up to?

Cursing and grunting, Will gave the handle a final

savage twist. Water gushed onto the floor and the swindler laughed uproariously. "Let's see what those mobsters have when I'm done with this place." He pounded his chest with his good hand. "I don't care what they say. They have no right to her. I cleaned out the filth, brought her back to her beauty. What did they do? Not a thing. They did nothin' except loan me some money. They didn't give their blood, sweat, and tears for this place." He sloshed through the water toward the steps. "If I can't have it, nobody will. I'll show those bastards. Hotel LaBelle is mine until death do we part."

What are you fixing to do now? Lucius followed behind Will, trying figure out how he could stop this idiot from ruining the hotel.

Up the basement steps the drunk stumbled, and continued to do so through the foyer, then into the elevator. He pressed the button and leaned against a wooden panel, panting, his eyes closed. When he arrived on the second floor, Will shoved the brass door aside and staggered down the hallway. He tripped, nearly fell, and righted himself with a curse. "Freaking area rugs."

Will yanked open the door to the barren white room and smiled.

"Ms. Tallulah, I gotta say, you're absolutely right. This room *is* ugly. Arctic, sterile, and barren. So stinking hideous, I'm going to get rid of it. And maybe myself while I'm at it." He grabbed a can of paint thinner, lay it on its side, and stabbed it repeatedly with a screwdriver. Sprinkling the acrid contents across the room, he placed the still draining can in the center of the mattress. Standing at the side of the bed, Will pulled a box of matches out of his pocket. Lucius recognized the matches as the same brand, perhaps even the same ones he used to light his cigar on his last night in the earthly realm. "This room won't be cold anymore. It's gonna be smoking hot."

Using his mouth to assist his good hand, Will slid the matchbox open and struck one against the side. The flame flared and fizzled.

"Crappy old things. Must be left over from Stewart." Another strike, another fizzle. Cursing a blue streak, he tried again.

Lucius grabbed Will's arm, to no avail. His ethereal fingers passed right through flesh and bone, making no impression on the boozed up man. Shouting, he attempted to get a message through, "Don't do this. Please!"

Forty matches in a box, Lucius calculated. How many had been left that day? He had smoked two cigars, and it had been a brand new box of phosphors. No reason to believe they were intact a century later. There might only be a few that worked out of what, ten or twenty?

"Aha!" the madman chortled and held up a flaming matchstick. "I give you fire!"

Lucius leaned over and blew as hard as he could.

The flame sputtered and disappeared.

"I did it," Lucius threw his head back and yelled to the ceiling. "I did it!"

The scratch of wood against wood stopped his rejoicing.

Another match flared.

Lucius huffed and it went out in a twist of smoke.

"Damn these things." Will struck another.

Lucius puffed and said, "I can do this all night, you

lunkhead. Give up."

Will bent over weeping and cursing. Lucius couldn't see what the other man was doing. The swindler's body blocked his view. He took a deep breath—and missed the glowing box of matches as they flew in the air and onto the bed—which burst into flames.

The desperate, drunken man cackled maniacally, burst into tears, and collapsed onto the floor.

The fire ate its way along the mattress cover, a hungry red demon eager for more fuel. It spilled down the side of the bed and traveled the path of the dribbled paint thinner over Will's inert body.

Lucius grabbed at a pillow to beat the fire out, but his fingers passed through it. He popped into the hallway. *Where is that gosh-darn new-fangled fire alarm?* The red-and-white square stood out in stark contrast against the dark wall.

Focus on the handle and do what the sign says. Pull.

Wispy, smoky, barely visible, his fingers passed through the handle, once, twice, three times without effect. He shrieked in frustration and despair. His life, if you could call it that, was over. If Hotel LaBelle went, perhaps he'd disappear too. Maybe the good Lord sent Will to punish him, over and above Beautiful Blackfeather's curse. Lucius loved his hotel, an inanimate object that made him puff up with pride like a rooster—so much so that he refused to leave it. He had loved the building more than he loved Mourning Dove.

Ruined, everything was ruined.

Chapter Eight

As night began to fall, Tallulah finished her dinner in silence, still recovering from her vision, and reflecting on how it differed from all the others. Aside from the highly interactive and extremely attractive Lucius, none of her other visions required her participation. The Pictograph Cave man, more like a moving, three dimensional photograph, disappeared before she could speak to him. She wondered if he'd ever appeared to any other visitors at the park. The ranger acted as though he'd never heard the story before.

The battlefield episode felt the same way, exploding around her, not only in three dimensions, but in full surround sound and chest-rumbling bass, like an immersive movie experience or video game. Both experiences had been impersonal, happening in front of or around her. According to experts on the paranormal, occurrences such as these were called residual hauntings. They played like tapes, over and over, whether people were there to see them or not. Someone born with the "gift," as her grandmother called it, would see these past events and people. From a more scientific perspective, some brains happened to be wired to receive these transmissions, like tuning into the frequency of a radio or TV station.

The vision today, however, had been personal. The

woman spoke directly to her and *only* her. The people offering Tallulah hospitality were descended from Beautiful Blackfeather. Yet, they could not see her. Neither did they "lead the witness" by identifying her, yet when Tallulah described her, they obviously recognized her immediately. It was almost as if the encounter had been anticipated...or intentional. How could they know she would be the right instrument to tune into the Beautiful Blackfeather station?

She swallowed her last spoonful of the delicious pudding, sipped her coffee, and placed her mug on a blue geometric coaster. Then she pinned Emma and her brother to their seats with her gaze. "How long have you guys been planning this?"

Bert glanced at Emma. "My sister called me, told me she thought you were the one——"

"I've been searching for the right person for years." Emma had the grace to blush. "I'm sorry I didn't tell you."

"This was a test?" Tallulah didn't know whether she should be angry or flattered.

Emma nodded and traced a pattern on the tablecloth. "Yes."

"Were you lying when you said you couldn't see Beautiful Blackfeather? 'Cause, if you were, you both deserve an Academy Award."

"No, we couldn't see her. Or hear her. We—ah— have other gifts," Bert said. He rolled his chair back and forth. "Our people are connected to horses in mystical ways, going back many centuries. My sister is a horse whisperer. That's why she changed her name from Blackfeather to Horserider. She communicates with the horses in their own language, breaks in broncos, and helps our rodeo people and Indian relay riders stay safe." He grinned. "Emma talks to dogs too but didn't want to be called the Dog Whisperer—that name was taken."

"What were you doing cleaning the hotel?" Tallulah knew it wasn't for the money. There had to be another reason.

"Keeping an eye on it for a friend." Emma stood and began to clear the dishes.

"Well, *that's* not cryptic at all." Tallulah sighed and pointed at Bert. "What about you? What's your talent?"

"Ha! If I told you, I'd have to kill you. Homeland Security and all that."

"Wow. You two are just a mystery wrapped in an enigma inside a puzzle, aren't you?" She drummed her fingers on the tabletop. "So what is it you want *me* to do, aside from communicate with your great-great-grandmother? You didn't seem at all surprised by her messages, so what's my purpose, really. And, please, don't go all national security on me. I'm not buying it."

Tail wriggling, Franny chose that moment to appear with a massive deer antler in her mouth. She dragged it over to Tallulah and placed it at her feet. "Whoa. Where did you get that?"

Emma waved to the trio entering through the dog door. "The other dogs must have given it to her."

"Given? Dogs don't normally give their toys away."

"She's a Medicine Woman's dog. They're showing her respect."

Tallulah squeezed her eyes shut. "I'm not a healer. I don't take care of sick people or even know anything about using plants for herbal medicine."

Emma placed a warm hand on her shoulder. "You see spirits who are sick and need your help. You lead them on the path to the camp beyond, what you call life after death, when they've lost their way. You walk on the path of light. Don't hide your gifts. We need your talents."

Her grandmother's warnings to keep her visions to herself didn't really apply here, did they? These people had unusual gifts too. They weren't looking to lock her up or drug her into a catatonic state, were they? She sighed. "Okay, I surrender. How can I help you? What is it you want me to do?"

"This won't hurt a bit." Bert chuckled.

Standing in front of the cabinet Beautiful Blackfeather had pointed to, Emma frowned at her brother and said, "Tallulah, could you come here, please? I need to show you something."

Emma pulled a drawer out and removed a bundle wrapped in deerskin. "This belonged to Beautiful Blackfeather. She told her family it was to go to the person who could see, hear, smell, touch, and taste the man she cursed, Lucius Stewart."

"How did you know—" She hadn't told Emma she'd kissed Lucius. Only the first four senses had been in their conversations.

"I saw your face when you spoke of him. It was only a matter of time before your lips met."

Heat filled Tallulah's face. "That was *all* we did." These two didn't need to know he'd rejected her advances and made her feel like piece of toilet paper on his shoe. "After all, what else could a ghost possibly do with a living woman?"

Emma snorted. "Let's not go there." She pointed to the recliner. "Since we don't know what will happen when you open this, you should probably lie down and get comfortable. I wouldn't want you to get hurt during this—experiment."

"That's the first reasonable thing you've said in the last five minutes." Tallulah sat on the chair, found the lever to raise her legs, and tried to relax. "Got a blanket? I might get chilly."

The other woman grabbed a soft throw covered with colorful geometric patterns and tucked it around Tallulah's legs. "Better?"

Bert pulled alongside her. "Good luck."

"Thanks. Okay, let's have it." She put her palms out to receive the bundle, expecting an electric shock or some jolt of supernatural *something* to hit her when it was placed in her hands. *Nothing.* She unwrapped the package with reverence, unwinding first the deerskin, then a cotton cloth, finally arriving at a—

"A stick with a white feather at the tip? This is the treasure of Beautiful Blackfeather?"

The siblings said nothing, just watched her with those big brown eyes. A melody, some old native music, filled the room. Were they humming? Or was it coming from outside?

"Okay, okay, I'll pick it up." She placed her hand over the stick, but before she could grasp it, the rod flew up and struck her palm as if someone had slapped it into her hand.

"Ouch!" No electric shock zapped her with a thousand volts. Instead, thunder clapped and a black vortex sucked her out of the cozy family room and into another space and time...

****

Tallulah arrived in Lucius Stewart's office, long before Will's ransacking. She scanned the room, expecting to see the dapper owner at his desk, but the chair stood empty. A cigar butt smoked in the ashtray, and a half bottle of whiskey sat on the desk next to an empty glass. She reached over to pick up some papers on the desk—and saw her mutilated arm. Slashed in numerous places, many of the wounds still oozed blood. She glanced down at her feet. Moccasins? No mirror, but the window might serve as one. She stood at the glass and peered at her reflection. Gone was the wild blonde hair. Instead, dark hair surrounded a sad-eyed, wrinkled face. Her hand went to the base of her skull of its own accord, and the stubble of close cropped hair met her fingers. She was in Beautiful Blackfeather's body. Now what? She stepped back to the desk and allowed Beautiful to take control.

The Medicine Woman picked up a document with scribbles and a thumbprint on it, along with a gold ring. Placing both into a small beaded buckskin bag, she walked outside to the river's edge and stripped. Everything, including her clothes, medicine stick, and small bag, went into the larger cloth pouch she carried on her back. Under the full white moon, she raised her hands and called upon her spirit animal. Shudders racked her body, bones cracked, and pain erupted along every inch of her as black-and-white feathers sprouted. Sharp talons now served as her feet, and her arms grew into wings. Dulled by the heavy drumbeat of her heart engulfed in grief, she felt no joy in shapeshifting.

Beautiful grasped the pouch in her sturdy claws

and launched into the night air. Below, the river chuckled, owls hooted, and mice rustled in the grass. No desire to dive into the water and pull out a fish thrilled her soul. The owls could have the mice. Tonight she mourned the loss of her only child and flew over the plains to the hulishoopiio, *the scaffolded sacred place where Mourning Dove's body lay wrapped in robes and ropes. Screaming her grief, she circled her daughter's grave three times and flew onward. She headed back to camp, back to her teepee where her infant grandchild, Mourning Dove's daughter, awaited her. It was time to be strong, to raise her daughter's child, a grandmother's grandchild, one without a mother or a father.*

Just as she was about to dive down to her home, an overwhelming urge to return to the white man's hotel overcame her. As she flew over the building, flames shot out of an upper window and a man screamed in pain...

****

Tallulah gasped and sat upright.

"She's back!" Bert shouted.

Emma's worried face hovered overhead. "Do you want some water or coffee?"

"I was in Beautiful's body—in Lucius' office. He wasn't there. I—she—took an important paper and a ring." She looked at her arms, threw off the blanket, and stared at her feet. Her voice fell to a whisper. "I—Beautiful turned into an eagle."

Bert placed his large hand over hers. "You're okay. You're here with us now."

"Lucius and Mourning Dove's daughter lived. You're her great-grandchildren and—" Panic gripped

94

her heart with the sharpness of an eagle's talons. "Fire! The hotel's on fire! Call the Sheriff! I have to get back there!"

"We'll make the call, but you can't go out in this thunderstorm. When it comes down this hard the roads wash out. You'll never make it."

****

Rain lashed the window and lightning flashed a staccato pattern in the pitch-black sky. Lucius paced the smoldering room and screamed in frustration, "I should be able to do something to save you, at least. You may be a scoundrel, swindler, and a deadbeat, but even you don't deserve this." He stood over the other man's inert form, his gaze wandering from head to foot.

Is that his itty-bitty phone next to him on the floor?

In his time, Hotel LaBelle boasted not only soft beds, fine dining, and good wine, but a telephone. When he built the hotel, he had installed a direct line from the train station to his registration desk, a business strategy that ensured a full house every spring, summer, and fall. He also paid the exorbitant fee of a dollar and two-bits a month for a party line so he could make and receive calls from local businesses and residents. Worth every penny. Now they had these palm-of-your-hand things. They still had numbers and he bet there was an operator in there, somewhere. He'd watched that scoundrel use the thing thousands of times, once he figured out what it was.

"Will, you bum, you ain't gonna die if I can help it."

He lay on top of the man like a second skin, and blew into Will's face, trying to keep the smoke away from his lungs. Between huffs and puffs, Lucius pressed the button and waved his palm over the glass like a magician. Nothing. He pressed the button harder and the cyclopean rectangle stared back at him.

If only Tallulah were here. Her presence made him more of a man, literally. What kind of idiot pushed a beautiful, smart woman like that away? Him, that's who. *Oh, Tallulah, I was a fool. If only I could right that wrong, make it up to you.*

He tapped at the button again. The screen lit up. He slid his fingers across the screen and a prompt told him to enter a passcode.

Must be like a secret password.

"For Heaven's sake. Could this be any harder?" He blew at Will's face. "Don't suppose you could tell me your passcode?"

No response from the man beneath him. Shallow breathing indicated he was still among the living, but Lucius didn't know for how long.

Keeping Tallulah's beautiful face in his mind, he repeated his efforts with the phone. This time, he saw the writing at the bottom of the screen. *Emergency.* If this wasn't an emergency, he didn't know what was. He pressed the word, and the rectangle turned white with an array of numbers. Now he was getting someplace. He pressed zero and an angel's voice answered.

"This is the mobile operator. What is your emergency?"

"Fire. Hotel LaBelle. Fire."

"I can hardly hear you, sir. Could you speak up please?"

He shouted as loud as he could, "Fire. Hotel LaBelle. Fire."

"I think I heard you say fire, Hotel LaBelle, is that

correct, sir?"

"Yes!"

"Where is the Hotel LaBelle, sir?"

Oh, for Heaven's sake. Wasn't this woman downtown in the Billings Exchange?

"Billings Montana!"

A siren wobbled in the distance. That was fast. She really was an angel.

"Thank you." The wailing came closer, and the crunch of tires on gravel, many tires, rose over the sound of the rain. A man shouted, "Get the hose in the river. Hook up the pump. Let's get this contained."

More shouts and siren shrieks came from below.

"Upstairs—the fire is upstairs. Search every room for survivors."

The floor trembled with the weight of many men, and the door slammed into the wall. Two men in dripping yellow suits, helmets, and masks stormed in.

"We've got a man's body."

"Grab him and get the hell out."

"Where's that water? Get that water up here!"

"Move, move, move!"

"More water, more water!"

Lucius followed the firemen outside to the porch. The rain had slowed to a drizzle, and the clouds scudded overhead, revealing a full opalescent moon.

"Give this guy some oxygen. Let's see if he's got a chance."

They placed Will on a stretcher inside a big red truck, and a young man with long dark hair pulled back in a ponytail slapped a clear mask on his face, then placed a stethoscope on Will's chest. "I've got a heartbeat and shallow breathing. I'm hooking up a normal saline IV." He slid open the window between where the stretcher sat and the front driver's compartment. "Check to see which ED is open. I'm hoping St. Vic's isn't on bypass."

The back doors slammed shut, and the ambulance raced up the driveway, tossing gravel and mud in its wake.

A burly man in yellow gear wore a helmet that said, "Captain." He spoke into a black box, "You guys find anyone else?"

A voice crackled out of the box, "Negative."

The captain nodded. "What's the status of the blaze?"

"Confined to this one weird-looking room. Paint's blistered, furniture's buckled, but the mattress must have been fire retardant. Windows and door were closed, so the fire didn't spread."

"I'm sure the rain helped, but it's still a miracle in a place this old." The captain shook his head. "Come out when you're confident it's extinguished. Be safe."

An hour later, five firemen emerged from the hotel.

"Hey, Captain, any idea who that guy was we found in the weird room?"

"No clue. Guess we'll find out after he gets to the ED."

One man held up Will's phone. "I'd like to know how he made an emergency call while he was unconscious."

The captain took off his helmet and scratched his bald head. "How do you know that?"

"The mobile operator was still on the phone when we entered the room." He handed the phone to his boss. "She said a man she could hardly hear called to report the fire five minutes before we arrived."

"But the Sheriff's office called us fifteen minutes before we got here."

"Exactly."

"I'll call the Sheriff and tell him we've got a mystery caller and a fire of suspicious origin. Time to call the arson investigator." The captain sighed. "Just once, why can't my job be easy?"

Lucius popped into the hotel, inspecting each room for himself, amazed at the limited damage. He approached the last room with trepidation. The ugly white room was now an ugly black room. Covered in soot and still dripping water, the boxy furniture stood on warped feet and looked as if one tap would knock it over. A large dark hole in the mattress gave mute testimony to the source of the conflagration. On the floor next to the bed, soot traced the outline of a man's body. Somehow, in the smoke and fire, Lucius had been able to keep Will alive. A miracle. Not that the man would be grateful if he ever woke up. He'd be facing arson charges and still dealing with owing the wrong men money.

He puzzled over the conversation he heard outside. Someone had called the Sheriff's office before he reached the operator. He gazed out the window into darkness. No one in their right mind would have been out in this downpour. The roads were impassable in those conditions. He hoped Tallulah hadn't been out driving during the thunderstorm.

Who could have known the hotel was on fire? How had *anyone* seen the glow out here in the middle of nowhere in the storm?

Chapter Nine

Tallulah clenched a tissue and waited while Emma made yet another call to the Sheriff's Office to get an update on the fire at the hotel.

"Emma knows everyone in the county," Bert said. "She went to school with the dispatcher, trained her horses."

"Oh, hello, yes, this is Emma Horserider. Can you tell me anything about the Hotel LaBelle fire? Really? Yes, oh that's great news. Uh-huh. Yeah. Oh *my*. Did you find Will Wellington? Is he okay? He did? Where is he now? Thank you very much, I really appreciate it."

"Good news?" Tallulah asked between sniffles.

"Yes. My Indian telegraph still works. The fire is out, and the hotel is mostly intact."

"What was the 'oh my' for?"

"Seems they can't figure out how Will survived the fire. The room was locked tighter than a drum, and the window was closed. Smoke should have done him in. Plus, someone made an emergency call from Will's phone five minutes before the trucks arrived." She gave Tallulah a pointed stare. "Any idea how an unconscious man could have done that?"

"Lucius," she said in a whisper. "Had to have been him."

Bert nodded. "Spirits love to tinker with phones

100

and lights."

"He wasn't playing—he was trying to save a man he despised." She shook her head. "His beloved hotel was in flames and—" She stopped, an image of a man in a window popping into her mind. "Lucius. He was the man I saw and heard screaming."

Emma pulled up a chair in front of Tallulah and handed her a mug of hot coffee. "This will help you shake off the trance state. That was another reason we didn't want you driving in the rain. Not safe to operate heavy machinery after a vision quest."

"Thanks." She blew on the surface and sipped. "You had the will. You're the rightful heirs, not that ass Will, Wilson, whatever his name is. Why didn't you guys assert your rights and take possession of the hotel? It belongs to you."

"We don't have the deed that proves Lucius paid off the mortgage."

"Ah." Tallulah reached into her blouse, pulled out the yellowed paper, and handed it to Emma. "Now you do."

Emma moved closer to Bert, and they both scanned the document.

Tallulah removed the throw, tossed back the rest of the coffee, and stood. "My work here is done."

"Not so fast." Bert put his hand up. "We need to talk about your vision."

"I told you everything. At first I was in my own body, then I let Beautiful take over and…"

"Beautiful wasn't in charge when you flew back over the hotel, was she?"

Tallulah shook her head. "No. I had an irresistible urge to go back, almost as if I was called back."

He pressed on, "And you saw the fire in real time."

"Yes. And heard the scream."

Bert patted the recliner. "Have a seat, my friend. We have business to discuss."

"That's my cue to leave." Emma put on a jacket. "This is top secret and I have horses to visit. Talk to you later, Tallulah."

Tallulah waved goodbye to Emma and plopped back down in the chair. Franny leaped on her legs, begging to be picked up. She pulled the pug to her lap and leaned back. "Okay, I'm listening."

Emma's brother rubbed his chin. "Ever hear of remote viewing?"

"No, can't say I have." She caressed Franny's velvet ear.

"The CIA had a program in the seventies to see if certain paranormal methods would have intelligence applications. Remote viewing was one of these activities. Researchers would ask someone like you to envision a place or object that a sender would be looking at. In other experiments, they would put a photograph into an envelope and ask the person to describe the picture. They did this in a variety of ways for about two decades."

A frisson of anticipation feathered along her spine. "What did they find?"

"A large evaluation study of the program found that, statistically, the results were positive. Remote viewers accurately described those places and objects more often than chance would suggest they should be able to."

"I'm no researcher but from my basic stats course in college, that means it worked, right?"

"Yes and no." Bert shrugged. "The statistics were good, but the intelligence wasn't detailed enough for practical uses in the field. They discontinued the program."

"Oh, that's disappointing." Tallulah wondered what this had to do with her.

"Yes and no."

"For someone who's so direct, you're certainly being coy." Tallulah shook a finger at him. "And I know your family secrets, so you shouldn't beat around the bush. What is it you want me to do *now*?"

"We live in extremely scary times, Tallulah. Every week, it seems, another extremist explodes a bomb. Homeland Security needs all the help we can get to prevent acts of terror."

"You don't have to tell me. I was in high school in Enid, Oklahoma when the Oklahoma City bombing occurred." She shuddered and Franny licked her hand. "It's burned in my memory."

Bert locked gazes with her. "Are you ready to serve your country?"

"I don't understand what you want me to do. I'm a hotel consultant who sometimes has visions. Not sure what good I would be."

"Tallulah," Bert scolded. "You're not just a 'hotel consultant who sometimes has visions.' You're a remote viewer. I want to train you to use your gifts to help protect our country."

"I don't know…" Her stomach fluttered.

"Listen, you were the one who said your visions were like uncontrolled seizures. I have people who can help you learn to control them, give you the power to turn them on and off at will."

"That would be nice." Her grandmother chirped in the back of her mind, but instead of saying, "Hide your gifts!" she shouted, "Take the job!"

"It would be undercover, part-time." He reached over and patted Franny's head. "You'd need to keep T & F Hotel Inspectors as your day job, so to speak."

Speaking half to herself and her grandmother, she said, "I don't know if I'm equipped for this kind of work."

"You've been ready for this job a long time. You just didn't know it."

She sighed. "Okay, I'll do it."

Bert reached over and grasped her smaller hand with his big one. "Welcome to Homeland Security, Tallulah. You're the newest employee of the Science and Technology Directorate, Anomaly Defense Division."

Emma burst through the door. "You done?"

Bert nodded. "All set."

"Good. Because she has one more thing she has to do, and she needs to do it soon."

An hour later, Tallulah and Emma stood outside the Hotel LaBelle under the luminous full moon. "Emma, I don't understand. Why couldn't *you* do this?"

"As she lay on her deathbed, Beautiful told my mother how she cast the curse. She pointed her medicine stick at him and said, 'You are cursed to stay in this dwelling that you love more than my daughter. You are cursed to wander it alone until you find someone you love and who loves you back, then and only then will this curse be undone.' When Beautiful realized he might never find someone, she knew she had been wrong to cast him into the world between worlds. She wanted to right the wrong, reverse the curse. But her medicine stick never sang for anyone before you."

"Lucky me," Tallulah said dryly. "Good thing I don't have to swear undying love. 'Cause that ain't happening."

Emma cocked her head to one side. "I thought you felt something for him."

Avoiding Emma's eyes, Tallulah stared at the hotel. "The feeling was not mutual."

"What?"

"We started to, you know, fool around." Heat flooded her face, and she was grateful for the dark night covering her embarrassment. "He called me a brazen hussy. So, I'm not feeling the love, if you get my drift."

"I apologize for my ancestor's behavior. What a jerk."

"Pretty much my thoughts. I gave him a lecture on women's rights. He was not impressed."

No sign of Lucius. She expected to see him pacing the porch or sitting in the rocking chair. "At any rate, I don't see him."

"You'll have to go in and find him."

Talk about awkward. The man rejected her, now she had to look for him to right Beautiful's wrong. *Would there be no end to this saga?* Yes, tonight was the last night she'd see him. After she undid the curse, he'd be free to move about the country or stay put and work with his descendants on a plan for the property. Either way, not her problem anymore. All she had to do was go in there, touch him with the medicine stick, and channel Beautiful Blackfeather, who, right this moment, stood at her side, petting Franny. The spirits loved her pug. Franny, the veritable ghost magnet.

The medicine stick hummed in the beaded quiver slung on her back. The magic wand's singing, she thought. It must be time. "Watch Franny for me?"

Tallulah handed the leash to Emma before she headed for the steps.

Still no sign of Lucius. Dang pesky spirit. He wouldn't leave her alone before, and now he wanted to play hide-and-seek? Tallulah pulled open the screen, and just as she put her hand on the front doorknob, tires crunched on the driveway and a siren whooped twice.

A megaphone enhanced voice shouted, "Step away from the crime scene."

Almost to the same second, the man she sought appeared in the etched oval glass on the other side of the door, and their gazes locked.

He grinned and popped onto the porch alongside her. "Looking for me?"

"Put your hands up, Miss. Step away from the door."

She put her hands up and turned to face the voice. Powerful searchlights blinded her and footsteps crunched in her direction.

"They don't seem happy to see you." Lucius poked her back, and she jumped. "Was it something you said?"

"Stop that," Tallulah hissed over her shoulder. "Can't you see this isn't a joking situation?"

"Can't help myself, I'm so happy to see you." He stroked her hair, and her knees turned to water. "Makes me say foolish things."

"Omigod, you have the *worst* timing."

The man with the megaphone continued, "Move

away from the door."

She shouted, "The owner invited me. I'm staying here."

A short, stocky deputy sheriff with dark hair bounded up the stairs, a huge roll of yellow tape in his big hands. "Not tonight you aren't. A man was beaten and almost died in a fire tonight. If you don't leave the premises, we will be forced to arrest you."

"That's not true," Lucius hissed in her ear. "I saw the whole thing. He set the fire. He tried to kill himself."

"Tommy Otterlegs, how *dare* you talk to my friend like that?"

"Oh, hi, Miss Emma. I didn't see you over there in the shadows." His glance bounced between Tallulah and Emma. "What are you doing here?"

"Didn't my friend just tell you she was invited here? She's a hotel inspector, hired to help Will figure out how to make a go of his business."

"Ha!" Otterlegs guffawed. "That's a good one. Will owed money to everyone. Looks like he managed to make someone mad enough to beat him to a pulp and set a fire to cover up the murder."

"I thought you said he *almost* died," Emma corrected. "Is it a homicide or not?"

He grinned. "Always the nitpicker, Emma, even in school. *Attempted* homicide. Is that better?"

"How is he doing? The dispatcher said he was in the ICU at St. Vic's."

"Sedated and on a ventilator, Emma." Otterlegs stretched yellow tape in an X across the door. "It's gonna be a while before we can question him." He grabbed Tallulah by the elbow and pulled her away from the door toward the steps. "You have to leave now, even if you were staying here. Maybe Emma can put you up for a while, at least until we get this wrapped up."

"That could take months," Tallulah protested, stepping back and yanking her arm away. "I need to get back in there and get to work. Will *really* needs my help now."

Tommy gave her a strange look. "You sweet on him?"

Her stomach roiled. "I make it a policy to *never* have romantic relationships with a client."

"Just the ghosts who wander the hotel," Lucius whispered at her other ear sending a thrill down her neck, and stirring up naughty responses from her nether regions. *He really knew how to torture her.*

"Miss Emma, can you take Miss—what is your name?"

"Tallulah Thompson."

"Take Miss Thompson to your place?"

"Sure, Tommy." Emma nodded. "She can come to the fair and watch the Indian relay races."

Tallulah stumbled down the steps, the medicine stick humming an angry tune for her ears alone. *Talk about bad timing.*

"Watch your step, Miss."

She walked toward Emma and looked back.

Otterlegs stretched multiple pieces of yellow tape between the handrails at the bottom of the stairs.

Lucius stood on the top step, shoulders slumped, palms out. He cried out, "Tallulah, I'm sorry I hurt your feelings. I'm sorry I called you a brazen hussy. I was wrong. More than wrong. I was a no-good, lousy saphead."

Tallulah's pulse skipped a beat, and she stood transfixed as the cop tried to urge her away from the hotel. She shook his hand off her arm. "Let me go."

"I learned my lesson. I would do anything to be with you. Anything."

Tears sprang to her eyes. Throwing caution aside, she shouted back, "I have no idea where this is going, Lucius Stewart, but I'm willing to take a chance on us." Reaching over her shoulder, she grabbed the medicine stick out of the quiver and ran for the steps.

Otterlegs said, "What the—" Footsteps pounded behind her. "I order you to stop!"

There was a loud thud and Emma said solicitously, "You okay, Tommy? You took a bad tumble."

"You tripped me!"

Tallulah reached the top step. She extended the vibrating medicine stick, touched Lucius on the nose, and spoke the Crow words Beautiful gave to her, then repeated them in English, "I forgive you. I undo this curse. I set you free."

Lucius shimmered and wavered. For a split second, Tallulah's heart rose into her throat, nearly choking her. What if she'd misspoken and he disappeared forever? Then the air around him rippled from his head to his toes, and he became solid before her eyes. He reached over the yellow tape and pulled her into a bone-crushing embrace. "You came back for me."

"You have no idea—"

"Put your hands up."

Lucius glanced over her shoulder. "Otterlegs has friends coming down the driveway."

Slowly, Tallulah turned, her hands up in the air, the

breath feather on the medicine stick waving slowly in the breeze. The rod no longer hummed. It had served its purpose.

"Step away from the hotel. Both of you."

"They can see me?" Lucius breathed behind her.

"The entire world can see you." She giggled in a fit of nerves. "Welcome to the twenty-first century."

Lucius raised both hands in the air, reached for hers, and squeezed. "Whatever happens, we're together now."

Otterlegs brushed at the mud on his uniform. "It's a simple job, they said. Won't take more than five minutes, they said. Get out here, seal the crime scene, and go home, they said." He reached for his handcuffs. "That's all I wanted to do."

"What are you doing, Tommy?" Emma called.

"My job. What's your name, mister?"

"My name is Lucius Stewart." Acutely aware of his century-old, pin-striped three-piece suit, suspenders, and silver bolero tie, he wished he wore clothes more in keeping with the times.

Otterlegs gave him a once over. "Yeah, right, and I'm Chief Plenty-Coups."

A black-and-white SUV with the Yellowstone County Sheriff's seal pulled alongside Tommy's patrol car. Two uniforms jumped out. "What's the deal, Otterlegs?"

"I think I've solved the attempted murder-arson case. Watch and learn, boys, watch and learn. Tallulah Thompson and Lucius Stewart, or whatever your real name is, you are under arrest."

Tallulah's stomach clenched. This could not be happening.

"Are you out of your mind, Tommy?" Emma shouted from the sidelines.

"Be quiet, Emma, or I'll arrest you for obstruction of justice." He smiled at Tallulah. "You have the right to remain silent. Anything you say can and will be used against you…"

Franny shrieked like a banshee and appeared at Tallulah's feet. The medicine stick quivered with fury. Fearful that Beautiful would appear and take matters into her own hands, Tallulah dropped the rod. Franny snatched it up before the cops could move and took off into the darkness.

"Emma," Tallulah called, "could you take care of Franny for me?"

"Don't worry," Emma replied. "She's in good hands."

The two cops led Lucius away to the SUV, and a metal band clenched around her heart. This was no way for him to re-enter society.

Otterlegs urged her into the back seat of the cruiser. "Watch your head."

I need to watch more than my head, she thought. The man of her dreams just popped into the twenty-first century without an instruction manual to guide him. *Lucius is going to need someone to watch over him—and it looks like it's going to be me.*

Chapter Ten

The booking officer opened the door to the holding cell. "Have a seat."

"I didn't get my phone call. I want a lawyer," Tallulah protested. "I know my rights."

The door clanged shut.

Out of habit, Tallulah kicked into inspector mode. A metal bench four feet long—too short to lie on, too uncomfortable to sit on for any length of time. Three cinderblock walls painted eggshell white. A concrete floor with a drain in the center that, if she could trust her nose, hadn't been cleaned in a long time. Or perhaps the pervasive stench came from the stainless steel sink and toilet combo? She walked over and examined the toilet paper roll.

"Lucky me. Someone left four squares." Glancing at the water-stained ceiling, she spotted the unblinking eye of a video camera monitoring her every move. *Just like Franny*. Tallulah stared at the toilet and decided she'd wait for her teeth to float before using it anytime soon.

She paced the perimeter of the confined space and considered her options. All the way in, she'd repeated her alibi, "I was with Emma Horserider all evening. You know her. Why won't you listen to me? Don't you want to know the truth?"

Otterlegs had just stared ahead and called into base

muttering a jumble of indecipherable ten-something codes.

"If you're going to talk about me, you could at least do it in English," she'd said.

Two hours later, she found herself in a urine-drenched cell, holding her blouse over her nose, taking shallow breaths. If she kept this up, she'd pass out soon, which might be preferable to the stench. Something shimmered in the corner and a figure emerged from the mist.

"Beautiful Blackfeather!" She dropped her collar in surprise. "What are you doing here?"

A smile wreathed the elder's face, and she signed, "Good man comes with a pipe. Smoke talk."

Shoes squeaked on concrete, and Beautiful vanished.

The clerk appeared at the bars shaking her head. "You must have a lot of juice. This is the fastest I've ever seen someone released from holding." She unlocked the cell. "Since you came in here with nothing but the clothes on your back, at least we don't have to worry about returning your property. Just sign these papers and you'll be on your way."

What on earth?

When she stepped out into the lobby, she discovered the reason for her quick release. Encircled by a small army of deputies, Bert Blackfeather held court, regaling the group with a Homeland Security story. "We followed the leads, ladies and gentlemen, that's good police work. The moral of the story is, let the evidence speak for itself. Don't assume you know what's going on. You know what assume spells, right? Making an ASS out of U and ME." The man with the peace pipe had arrived to negotiate.

A round of laughter.

"There she is." He turned to the crowd. "I need some time with my client. Be safe out there."

He rolled over to a corner and motioned for Tallulah to have a seat in one of the orange plastic chairs. What was it about the color orange and jails?

Shaking from fatigue and stress, she shuffled across the room, struggling to understand the legality of his springing her out of jail—well, pre-jail. "I'm your client? How is that possible?"

"Don't look so surprised." He pulled out a business card. "Got my JD before I went to work for Homeland. Member of the Montana bar, along with DC, Maryland, Virginia, and a variety of other states. Comes in handy when my employees get their tail feathers in a bind."

"Lucky for me." She glanced around. "Where's Lucius? Are they bringing him here too?"

"Ah, Lucius is another matter." Bert shook his head. "He had no ID, so despite the fact that Emma vouched for him, Otterlegs decided my ancestor was a person of interest."

"Is he in a holding cell too? Can't you get him out?"

"Deputy Sheriff Otterlegs is an ambitious little man. Wants to make a name for himself, run for Sheriff. At the moment, our short-legged friend is working on charging documents." Bert smiled. "The good news is he became very annoyed when I told him I was Lucius's lawyer. The bad news is Will Wellington is still unconscious in ICU at St. Vic's. We have no way to disprove Otterlegs' charges of attempted homicide and arson."

"Yes we do!" Anger at the twerpy little deputy bubbled up. Lucius wasn't even around when it happened. "I saw those hoods who came to beat the snot out of him. Saw them, their vehicle, *and* their handiwork. I spent a lot of time putting ice and frozen peas on that man's injuries."

Bert rubbed his chin. "Any idea why they went after Will?"

"He said something about not being able to pay the 'vig.' I have no idea what that is."

"Oh-ho! A loan shark had him by the balls." He slapped his thigh. "Vig is a street term for interest. Most people who get a loan from a mobster can't pay the loan off, unless they win the lottery. Instead, they pay a weekly fee, like interest. If you get behind on the vig, they send very strong reminders."

"These two reminders had no necks, lots of tattoos, metal-tipped cowboy boots, and Nevada plates."

Bert tapped the screen of his cell phone and smiled. "Do you think you could pick them out of a photo array?"

"A what?"

"A line up. Mug shots. It's all digital now." He held his index finger up and grinned. "Hal, sorry to call so late. Did I wake you up? Oh, you weren't sleeping? That's lucky. Yes, I'm in for the fair, but I've got a situation." He gave a brief rundown to the person on the other end of the line. "That's great. I appreciate it. Thanks very much. Give my best to the wife."

"Who was that?"

"The Yellowstone County Sheriff. One of my best friends from high school. He will *personally* meet with us in the morning to hear what you have to say." Bert chuckled and rubbed his hands. "Otterlegs will learn not to piss on the big dog when you're the little dog. You must be starving. There's a great all night café not too far from here. Hope you like Mexican."

Tallulah felt guilty going out to eat while Lucius remained locked up with God-only-knew what kind of animals. Her heart ached for him. He had been in limbo for a century, wasn't that a long enough sentence for any man? They couldn't get him out soon enough. The world had changed over the last hundred years. Both the crimes and the criminals had gotten worse, more vicious. The poor man must be so overwhelmed and confused. Lucius came from a genteel time. He'd never make it in a jail full of toughs.

****

"What is your legal name, address, birthdate, and emergency contact person, medical and mental history?"

The series of questions sounded like one long run-on sentence to Lucius's ears. After jotting down the answers, the male booking clerk took Lucius's thumb and rolled it inside the blue square.

"Try to relax. When you tense up, your swirls flatten and your fingerprints won't come out right."

Lucius looked askance at the lanky man with the long brown hair. "I'm in the hoosegow for something I didn't do and you're saying I should be worried about my 'swirls' and think happy thoughts?"

"When you put it that way…" the clerk's lips quirked.

"This is all a mistake. I didn't hurt anyone. He's alive because of me."

"If I had a nickel for every guy who told me that, I

could retire. Stand here. Hold this sign with your name and ID number. Look straight at the camera." A flash of light made Lucius see spots. "Now turn your head to the left. No, the other left." The second flash nearly blinded him.

"Now what?" Lucius blinked to get rid of the stars.

"Time for your shower and your new duds." The clerk handed him a bar of soap. "I'll put your belongings in a bag and label them. If you ever get out of here, you'll get them back."

Scrubbed and shivering, Lucius pulled on the slate-colored uniform. The pants were five inches short of his sandaled feet. "Got a pair that fits?"

"You're a real comedian, aren't you?" The booking clerk pointed at a black phone on the wall. "You get one call."

Lucius picked up the phone and waited. "What's this buzzing sound?"

The clerk grabbed the receiver and held it to his ear. "It's a dial tone. What's wrong with you?"

"How do I reach the Billings Exchange?"

"The what?" The man's mouth fell open. "You mean to say you don't know how to use a phone?"

"Of course I do," Lucius retorted. "This one's different from mine, is all."

The clerk shook his head. "Obviously, smartphones didn't make *you* smart."

"I need to call my friend, Tallulah Thompson. She'll help me."

"You got a number for this person?"

Lucius shook his head.

"Then we're done here."

The clerk pointed the way down the hall.

"Attempted murder and arson. You'll fit in just fine with these boys. You'll find it's a bit crowded. Supposed to have one hundred and forty-seven inmates. As of today, we're up to four hundred and sixty-four. Even our women's areas are full up—and we have a baker's dozen of cranky female inmates sleeping on portable beds in the day room. Heard we're gonna ship some out to Valley Detention Center." He shook his head. "No room at the inn."

"I'd be happy to make reservations at another hotel," Lucius said.

"Ha! You're funny." The clerk handed him sheets, towels, and a blanket, then passed him off to a corrections officer. "Your personal CO is here to introduce you to the boys. If you don't like your accommodations, you can send an email to our customer service representative."

"What's an email?"

The clerk walked away laughing.

The CO grabbed the door handle and spoke into a black box on his shoulder, "Control, could you open the door, please?"

Something buzzed and the CO yanked the heavy metal door open. "I'll show you to your cube—we ran out of cells, no private suite for you.'"

A wave of noise hit Lucius like a body blow, followed by a barrage of sweat, urine, and feces assaulting his nostrils. He tried to cover his ears, but the handcuffs only allowed him to cover one. Taking a deep breath, he shuffled through the entryway. Behind him, the door clanged shut. Everywhere he looked men in identical uniforms lounged on white chairs or stood in knots talking—all staring at him. The CO uncuffed him and pushed him forward, a ripple of snickers following his path.

A large Asian man with close-cropped hair and a tear drop tattooed on his face sneered at him. "What's the matter, big boy? You afraid of us?"

Just like the drunks in New York City and the cowboys in Billings, he thought. Always looking for a fight. *Buncha roosters scratching at the dirt*. This was no time to show fear. Lucius shrugged. "Well, that depends. Do I fight one of you at a time or all of you at once?"

"Hey," the CO shouted. "Knock it off. No fights. You start a fight, you're gonna look at four walls in solitary for a long time."

"Aw, if you do that we won't be able to have the welcome committee visit him." The Asian put his palm to his face and batted his eyes.

Lucius's gaze snagged on three circular burn scars on the back of the man's hand. "You should watch where you put out your cigarettes."

Anger sparked in the man's eyes, and his nostrils flared. "Watch your back, bro, or you're gonna have a rough stay."

"That's enough, Nguyen." The CO led Lucius to a cube with walls that went up to his hips. A cot with unidentifiable brown stains awaited him. "Here you are, cube twenty-eight. A word of advice, my friend. That guy is on his way to the state prison, a lifer. He'd just as soon kill you as look at you. He doesn't give a crap. Keep your head down, and pray you make bail before you get hurt."

Lucius nodded. "Thanks for the tenderfoot talk. I'll try to be overcareful, keep my flap shut."

"Chow's on at seven in the morning. Grab a tray full of food and find a table. Avoid the skinheads and the Asians."

"What about the Crow? Can I sit with them?"

The CO stared at him. "If they *let* you." He shook his head. "Good luck. Hope you last the night."

After making up his cot, Lucius sat and stared at his new abode. He'd seen a lot of things in his one hundred and thirty-five years, but this beat all. The city of Billings had built a courthouse and jail just two years before Beautiful cursed him. He was pretty sure that hoosegow didn't hold more than a dozen men. Where had all these outlaws come from? Most of them looked young, and almost all of them wore tattoos. What did they mean?

A head popped over the wall. The kid couldn't have been more than eighteen. His skinny, pasty-colored face was covered with oozing sores, and his eyes bulged. "You want some *personal* services?"

"What in the Sam Hill are you talking about, kid?"

The youngster looked confused. "My name's not Kid. It's Ryan."

"Well, Ryan, what do you want?"

"Your soup, maybe your roll? The big guys steal my food. I'm hungry. I'll work for food."

Lucius inspected the cubicle. "Don't need a handyman."

The kid slid around the wall. "If not a hand, what about a mouth? Or—"

The penny dropped and Lucius jumped to his feet. "Get outta here before I thrash you."

The kid slunk away.

He lay back on his cot and stared at the ceiling.

Sagging tiles with coffee-colored stains he guessed were from a leaking roof bowed down, threatening to fall.

"Lights out." Spotted with small glowing lights, the room fell into darkness.

Lucius bunched his blankets up and crawled under the cot. He might be a tenderfoot, but he wasn't a fool. After about an hour, shuffling drew near. How many. Two, three? He held his breath. Muffled pounding on the cot and muttered curse words. A ripping sound. Time to stand up for himself.

Roaring like a bear, Lucius sat up and threw the cot aside. The dim light revealed a blanket covered form. A kick to the groin toppled that one. Someone jumped on his back and put a sharp tip to his throat. He tossed that one like a rag doll and took pleasure at the sound of a bone cracking on the hard walls. Just as the third one came at him, the lights blazed on, and the room filled with deputies and corrections officers.

"Back to your bunks," crackled a voice from on high. "Stand down."

Panting, Lucius stood in his cubicle, gratified at the sight of two thugs at his feet, one still grabbing his crotch and moaning. The other's forehead sported a nice gash and poured blood down the side of his face onto the floor. Both Asian men wore black panther tattoos and tear drops under their eyes.

A corrections officer examined the bleeder and called for assistance. "We need to get this one to the dispensary. He's gonna need stitches."

The officer who originally escorted Lucius to his bunk stood with his fists on his hips. "Didn't I tell you to lay *low*?"

"Yes, you did and I thank you for that good advice." Lucius winked. "I do believe you saved my skin. I hid under the cot, just like you said."

The CO shook his head. "With any luck, that gang will leave you alone now."

"You gonna put me in solitary?"

"If I had a cell, I would. As it stands even those are full, so I have no place to put you." He shook his head. "Over half these idiots are in here on alcohol or drug charges. If we could get the heroin addicts and meth heads out of here, we'd reduce the population by twenty percent."

"Used to be," Lucius offered, "the Sheriff would toss them in the drunk tank, let them out after they slept it off."

The CO stared at him. "Drunk tank? You talk like you're from another century."

Lucius nodded. "That would be correct. I told that guy up front my birth-date. Had to repeat it three times. November tenth, eighteen-seventy. I suspect he didn't believe me."

"Oh, great." He keyed his radio. "Control, would you please let the jail commander know we need a shrink for our latest guest. He thinks he's over a hundred years old."

Laughter erupted from the black box. "Ten-four. I'll let him know."

He gave Lucius a penetrating stare. "Try to stay out of trouble, okay? We lost a guy last year. Publicity was a nightmare. We keep telling the commissioners we need more space and more help. They don't listen." He walked away shaking his head. "Eighteen-seventy."

Lucius sank down on his sagging cot and put his

back against the wall. He'd see them coming if they tried again. Minutes, then hours passed by. Not much different from his time at Hotel LaBelle, he thought. Less interesting scenery than the river. Through slits of windows at the top of the wall, he watched the sky changing from midnight black to pre-dawn gray. Despite his best intentions, his eyes drooped. He shook himself awake, only to drowse again a few moments later. Someone slid onto the bunk next to him and touched his leg. He was wide awake again.

"For Heaven's sake, Ryan, I told you no." He turned to push the pesky kid off the cot and came nose to nose with the love of his life.

"Mourning Dove?"

Chapter Eleven

After a night of tossing and turning on a lumpy mattress at a low budget motel followed by a complimentary breakfast of tepid coffee and powdered eggs, Bert's early morning call came as a welcome relief. "Thanks for picking me up." She climbed into Bert's specialized van. "Emma sent me a video of Franny playing with her dogs. She won't want to come home with me."

Bert smiled. "I told you. Dog Whisperer."

Tallulah glanced out the window at downtown Billings. She'd read the magazine in the room promoting the town and learned a bit, including the fact that every night was two for one ladies night at the Grub Pub. Despite the battlefield, and the presence of Montana State University, this was neither a vacation nor a college town. The place had a population of slightly over one hundred thousand, where people lived, worked, and raised families. Art galleries perched alongside restaurants, and splashes of colorful modern paintings nestled between turn of the century red brick buildings. They passed a large bank, the combo police department and courthouse, and pulled into a public parking lot. Which reminded her that she needed to get her rental back.

"I hope my car is still out at the hotel—and that they'll let me have it."

"You haven't been charged with any crimes, so I'll raise a ruckus if they try to keep you from picking it up." Bert flicked a switch that opened the side door, transferred into his wheelchair, and hit a button which lowered the lift. "The Sheriff's meeting us in his office. He'll get us set up in a room to look at the mug shots online."

"Any chance we could get a cup of coffee along the way?" Tallulah climbed out of the van. "The light brown water at the motel didn't measure up to my caffeine standards, and I'm pretty sure my mattress was a bag of rocks."

"Hal's secretary will keep it coming." He pressed the key fob, and the van sealed itself up with a chirp. "I used to date her in high school. She knows exactly how I take my coffee."

"Is there anyone in Billings that you and Emma *don't* know?"

He laughed. "The tourists."

The automatic door whooshed open, and Bert greeted every person they passed from the janitor to the deputies. The Sheriff's secretary, a heavyset brunette with big brown eyes and a bit too much makeup, batted her lashes at Bert. "Hey there handsome, you in for the fair?"

"You betcha. And a little legal business. Hal around?"

"Right here," a voice boomed from behind. "You taking roll call?"

Dressed in a black uniform, a tall, lean man with gray hair and a mustache slapped Bert on the back, and then gripped Tallulah's hand. "You must be my witness."

"Tallulah Thompson. Yes, I saw the men who attacked Will Wellington." Her heart sped up, and her mouth went dry. "Have you seen my friend, Lucius Stewart? Is he okay? Can I visit him?" After his hundred year solitary confinement at the hotel, she worried he hadn't fared well in crowded captivity.

Hal motioned them into his office. Awards, citations, and plaques attesting to his bravery, honor, and civic works covered every inch of the walls. He pointed to a seat.

"Delilah, coffee for my guests, please."

"I'm on it, Boss." She walked in the room with a tray and condiments.

Tallulah took a cup with shaking hands. "Thank you, thank you, thank you."

"It's not that stuff you get down the street from the fancy place, but it'll get your heart jump started."

She took a deep gulp and sighed. "So, about my friend?"

"He's fine, made it through the night without getting killed, which is saying something." Hal shook his head. "Your buddy made the mistake of smart mouthing an Asian gang-banger."

Her heart leaped into her throat. Her worst fears had come true. Lucius was a kind, gentle man. He had no experience when it came to thugs. "Is he okay?"

"Him? He's fine. Fortunately for him, he's in good shape. He put one guy in the hospital and another will be walking funny for a while." He sipped his coffee and gave her a hard stare. "Does he have a history of mental illness?"

"Why do you ask?" Her pulse raced, and her mind went right to her grandmother's tales of psychiatric hospitals and zombie-shuffle-inducing drugs. "He seemed perfectly lucid to me."

"He told the booking clerk he was born in eighteen-seventy, and that he was the owner of the Hotel LaBelle."

She gulped her coffee and stared at the chipped wooden desk.

Bert jumped into the silence. "Oh, he's a kidder. You know the original owner of the Hotel LaBelle had the same name. He was pulling someone's leg."

Hal shook his head. "The owner, Will Wellington, is in the ICU holding on by a thread. It's a miracle he didn't die from smoke inhalation, not to mention his injuries."

"Let me tell you about those injuries—and the men who did it to him." Tallulah recounted seeing the black SUV with the Nevada license plate come and go, then Will's condition when she found him, as well as the pill bottle from Vegas with the other name on it. "He was a mass of bruises and cuts. Said they slammed his hand in a drawer."

"Why didn't you call us?" Hal frowned. "That's what we're here for."

"I wanted to." She put the empty paper cup down, wishing Delilah would wander in with another. "Will told me it would make more trouble for him. Said he couldn't pay the vig and some mobster from Vegas sent them out to, uh, encourage him."

"Hard to get blood from a turnip," Bert said. "That guy—his name isn't really Wellington, by the way—owes money to everyone, including my sister."

Hal grimaced. "Jeez, you really don't want to piss *her* off."

"Exactly." Bert slapped his thigh. "So, what do you think?"

"You seem like a credible witness." He nodded. "What was Wellington's other name?"

"Thomas Wilson, from Las Vegas," Tallulah said.

"I'll run it through the FBI database, see if anything pops up. Meantime, Delilah will take you down the hall to review the mug shots. One of our deputies will assist you."

"Not Otterlegs, I hope," Bert said.

"I do believe Deputy Otterlegs is out looking for a guy who failed to appear in court." Hal rolled his eyes. "God only knows when he'll be back."

A female deputy with red hair pulled up in a bun met them in the hall. "Come with me, please." She showed them how to search the records, local, county, state, and federal, then left them alone. "Need anything, just holler for Wanda. I'll be next door."

"I wish we could search on tattoos. I'm pretty sure I'd recognize the patterns."

"I'm sure that's a different database." Bert rolled over, closed the door, and dimmed the lights. "I'd like to try something, if you don't mind. It could speed things up."

"Sure, anything to help."

"I want you to do a remote viewing."

"Here? Right now?" She wasn't sure she could do it without some added power. "Don't I need Beautiful's medicine stick?"

"Did you have it when you experienced all those other visions?"

She shook her head. "No."

"Close your eyes, take a deep breath, lean back in

the chair, and think about the men from that day. Can you see them?"

Tallulah settled back in the chair, allowed her head to drop back, and closed her eyes. Franny, per usual, was taking her sweet time, checking every blade of grass and each flower. A car roared up and doors slammed. The two enormous thugs emerged into view.

"Yes, they're wearing muscle shirts that are too tight, as if they'll tear them off in a wrestling match." She took a deeper breath. "One is taller than the other. He holds his back stiff and straight, reminds me of a military bearing. His neck, so tan, looks like leather." She tilted her head for a better view of his hands. "His index finger and the thumb on his left hand—they're gone." A flash caught her memory's eye. "He's wearing a diamond earring. Left ear."

"Terrific, you're doing well. They get in their car…"

"A cloud of dust and gravel kicks up." Suddenly, she floated in the air over the car, tracking its progress. "They drove to the highway and headed south." The plains and mountains blurred, and she found herself over the vehicle, which drove on a busy street. The night was dark, but the flashing lights and billboards made it as bright as day. The thugs climbed out of the SUV and tossed the keys to a valet standing in front of a podium emblazoned with the name of a hotel. "Ohmigod." She sat bolt upright. "They're in Vegas. At the Glynn."

"Excellent work!" Bert grinned. "Let's take a look at the Nevada mug shots and see if we can find our friends."

An hour later, she shouted, "That's them. The same

tattoos. A globe with an eagle over it. Semper Fi. There's that military background. The Smith brothers."

"Guess they don't make cough drops." Bert stared at the screen. "John and Michael. What did they do?"

"Assault."

"Well, at least they're consistent." Bert opened the door and yelled, "Wanda!"

****

Inmates chattered in a cacophony of sound that drowned out his astonished exclamations. The morning sunlight slanted across his dead lover's regal features.

"Darlin' Dovie, I've missed you so much." Lucius reached out to caress her cheek, but his hand passed through her face. A pang of disappointment pierced his heart. The woman he once longed to marry sat next to him but in a different world.

Mourning Dove curled her arms together and rocked them.

"The baby." Tears sprang to his eyes, and his throat clogged. "I know. You lost the child."

She shook her head so hard, her braids whipped around. She signed two fingers walking on her hand, then raised one palm high.

"The baby grew up?" His voice quivered. "Our child lived?"

She smiled, nodded, put her hands over her heart, and disappeared.

"I'm a father!" He jumped up and shouted to anyone who would listen. "I'm a daddy!"

Laughter, hoots, epithets, and jeers greeted him. Bubbling with joy, he plopped down on the cot, closed his eyes, and wrapped his arms around himself.

The floor shuddered with heavy footsteps, and he

felt the presence of giants. He opened his eyes. Two bronze-skinned, long-haired men with tree trunks for legs stood in front of him.

"You Lucius Stewart?" the larger of the two titans asked.

Reluctant to open his mouth for fear of squeaking out his assent, he nodded.

The other one reached down and pulled him up by the elbow. "I'm Jimmy; this is Tommy."

"Stick with us. In here, we're your clan."

Had they heard him talking to Mourning Dove? Did he dare to dream they might be related?

The bigger one nodded. "Bert Blackfeather is your friend; we've got your back."

Who's Bert Blackfeather? Had to be related to Beautiful, but how?

He glanced around the room. The big, tough Asian guy and his gang were busy looking at the floor, the walls, their shoes, everywhere but at Lucius. A wave of relief mixed with uncontrollable mirth rolled through him. These giants weren't his great-great-grandchildren. They were his new gang.

Two hours later, after a breakfast of stale bagels and tepid dishwater they called coffee, a deputy shouted his name over the hubbub.

"Lucius Stewart. Front and center."

Accompanied by his new best friends who cleared the path ahead of him, Lucius made his way to the deputy.

"Time for your arraignment. The video system is down, so we're taking you into the courtroom." He held up cuffs and shackles. "Your jewelry."

Jimmy nodded and extended his hands, indicating

how Lucius should cooperate. "Don't worry, man. As long as they don't make you run, you'll be fine."

"Thank you, Jimmy. Tommy. See you back here?"

Tommy nodded. "Bert's a good lawyer. He's not in town often, so count your blessings he's here to help you."

After a short, uneventful ride in a van with nine other jailbirds, all of whom needed a bath, a deputy gripped his elbow and shuffle walked Lucius out of the van, into an elevator, and up to the second-floor courtroom. Two rows of prisoners sat along one wall, like naughty parishioners waiting for the minister to start preaching. The bailiff cried, "All rise, court is in session, the Honorable Judge Joseph Williams presiding."

A balding man with wire-rimmed glasses and long black robes appeared behind the judge's bench. "Be seated." His gaze passed over the room, and he shook his head. "I see we have an unusually large crop of cases today, over a hundred on my docket. You're keeping our law enforcement officers busy. Must have been a good weekend."

A titter of laughter rolled through the courtroom.

"Today, after we get through the juveniles—and I see there are only three—I've decided to start with the fellow with the worst charges. That means you drunk, disorderly, failures to appear, and other assorted lesser charges are going to have to kick back and wait your turn."

The inmates looked around as if trying to figure out who that lucky first one might be. Lucius craned his neck too and spotted Tallulah in the second row of wooden benches. A man in a wheelchair who wore a tiny American flag on his suit jacket lapel sat in the aisle next to her. Lucius raised his hands and waved his fingers at Tallulah. She gave him the thumbs-up sign.

At least one of them was optimistic.

Other than the fatigue on her face and her wrinkled clothes, she looked good. So good, his heart gave a little stutter jump, and he felt a smile crack across his face in spite of his dire situation. One thing for sure, he did not miss being under that curse, a spirit without a form, unable to feel his surroundings. She changed—no—*transformed* him into a real man, maybe even a better man than he'd been with Mourning Dove.

Mourning Dove. The memory of her face, so close to his this morning, made him to want to weep. Beautiful Blackfeather had forgiven him—but how could he forgive himself for not letting go of a pile of wood to be with the woman he loved? How could he forgive himself for letting her die? Somehow, he *had* to find the descendants of that child—his child—and make amends.

He jerked upright at the sound of his name being called. A deputy hauled him out of his seat and led him over to a table in front of the judge. The man in the wheelchair was already there, making notes on a yellow pad. Another man in a suit sat at a similar table on the other side of the aisle.

The judge cleared his throat and gave Lucius a hard stare. "This is Yellowstone County DC 13, State of Montana vs. Lucius Stewart, Judge Joseph Williams presiding. The Defendant Lucius Stewart is present in court with Defense Counsel Bert Blackfeather. The State is represented by County Attorney Robert Miller. You may be seated, Mr. Stewart."

Hands at his waist, Lucius planted himself in the chair and looked at his lawyer for guidance.

"Keep your eyes on the judge."

He nodded and obeyed.

"Mr. Stewart, we are here today for an Arraignment Hearing," Judge Williams continued. "The purpose of the hearing is to notify you of the criminal charges pending against you in this court, and your rights with regard to these charges. You have a right to remain silent. Anything you say can be used against you, including as evidence at trial. If you are unsure of how to respond to any question, you may consult quietly with your attorney before responding."

He leaned over to Bert and whispered, "I didn't do anything."

Bert nodded. "Hang in there. Just be honest."

"Mr. Stewart, today, are you under the influence of alcohol or any drug that clouds your judgment?"

"No, Your Honor, I am not." The only thing clouding his judgment was his complete confusion about what he was doing here.

"Are you suffering from any physical or mental condition that interferes with your ability to understand today's proceedings?"

"No, sir, I am not."

Hurried whispers between a deputy and Miller caused the judge to pause.

"Mr. Miller, do you have something you wish to say about Mr. Stewart's ability to understand today's proceedings?"

"No, Your Honor."

"Let us proceed, then." The judge rustled some papers. "Have you received a copy of the charging document?"

Bert held up a paper. "We have, Your Honor. I'm giving a copy to my client as we speak."

"Is your legal name Lucius Stewart, as set forth in the caption of the charging information?"

"Yes, sir, it is."

"Have you read the charging information?"

"No, sir."

"Take a minute to review it, please."

An excellent reader, Lucius nonetheless took more time than he needed.

This is insane. I didn't do any of this. Metal cuffs rattling, he put his hands down and nodded.

"Do you understand the allegations set forth within the information document?"

"Yes, Your Honor."

"Based on your understanding, do you waive having the document read to you now?"

"I do."

"In summary, as stated in the document, you are charged with three offenses. Count one, aggravated assault. Count two, arson. Count three, deliberate homicide, should the victim die. These crimes were allegedly committed on or about yesterday within Yellowstone County, Montana." The judge shook his head. "Should the victim die, the offense of deliberate homicide is punishable by life imprisonment or death. Should the victim live, the offenses of aggravated assault and arson are each punishable by a maximum of twenty year's incarceration at Montana State Prison and a fine of not more than fifty thousand dollars."

He felt like a character in a dime novel, one where the good guy is actually the bad guy and vice versa. The more the words rolled over and around him, the more a rock pile of despair weighed on his chest. Soon, he'd be crushed with the weight of the words falling down on him. "In addition to the penalties I have already stated, if you plead guilty or are found guilty you are subject to obligations for payment of restitution for the financial loss suffered as a result of the offenses and costs, fees, and financial assessments that come as part of a conviction."

Money. They want money? Good luck with that. Hysteria bubbled up and he bit the inside of his mouth to keep from laughing.

"In answering the charges you have rights." The judge read through the script of rights, including keeping silent.

I've been silent long enough. The urge to shout out his innocence battled with his need to show respect to the court.

"With your rights in mind, are you ready to enter a plea to the charged offenses?"

Bert nodded. "Yes, we are, Your Honor."

"Please stand, Mr. Stewart."

He rose to his feet, legs as wobbly as a new foal. How could he get through this without collapsing? A newborn to this world in most respects, how would he find his way? He had to rely on Blackfeather and Tallulah, he guessed. For that, he offered his gratitude to the good Lord for bringing them into his life.

"Mr. Stewart, to the charges of aggravated assault, arson and deliberate homicide, how do you plead, guilty or not guilty?"

His mouth dry, he croaked, "Not guilty."

"The record will reflect a 'not guilty' plea to the

offenses in the charging document. Does the defense seek to have a trial date selected today?"

Bert nodded. "Yes, we do, Your Honor."

With the assent of both attorneys, the judge moved on to the bail hearing.

"Mr. Stewart, the purpose of this hearing is to determine the necessary and appropriate conditions for your release from jail pending trial. Has the State prepared a proposed release order with release conditions?"

The County Attorney stood. "Commensurate with the nature of the offenses charged and with the fact that we feel the defendant poses a serious flight risk—he has no identification, is unemployed, and just appeared in town yesterday—we recommend the defendant not be released. We want him held in custody, without bond to ensure he makes it to trial."

"Has the Defendant reviewed the release conditions proposed by the State?"

"We have, and we disagree, Your Honor."

Lucius wanted to hug Bert.

The judge threw his glasses down on his desk. "Please state your arguments regarding release conditions and bail."

"Mr. Stewart has no prior record and has deep-rooted connections with the Billings community. He left as a young man and returned yesterday to be reunited with his family, which is why he 'just appeared' as Mr. Miller said. His belongings were stolen from him, which is why he had no identification when he was arrested."

"Where are his family members?"

"You're looking at them, Your Honor."

"Is this some kind of joke, Mr. Blackfeather?"

"No, sir. We're...cousins, on my great-grandmother's side, once removed."

"I know you're a competent lawyer, Mr. Blackfeather and there's no law against an attorney representing a family member. But, this isn't a movie. Mr. Stewart, are you *certain* you want your cousin to represent you?"

"Yes, sir."

The judge shook his head. "Go on. What do you propose?"

"Release him to my family. He can stay with my sister, Emma Horserider."

"Hmmm." The judge pinched his nose. "What do you say to that, Mr. Miller?"

"This is highly unusual, Your Honor." Miller's eyes bugged out, and the veins in his neck bulged. "Ever since he was arrested, this man has been claiming he was born in eighteen-seventy and that he's over a century old. He's not *competent* to leave the jail."

The judge put his palm out. "Hold on a moment. Mr. Miller, when Mr. Stewart said he had no conditions that would interfere with his ability to understand the proceedings that was your opportunity to disagree. Yet you said nothing about these assertions. Now you're saying he's mentally ill? You can't have it both ways. Whose side are you on?"

Miller's mouth opened and closed like a fish out of water.

"Hearing no further objections and considering the gravity of the alleged offenses, I hereby grant bail at the amount of five hundred thousand dollars. Can your cousin post the required amount?"

Bert nodded. "Yes. We take care of our family. We will post his bail, Your Honor."

Miller threw his hands in the air. "This is absurd. Where are you going to get that kind of money?"

Bert stared daggers at the opposing counsel. "That's my family's business, not yours."

The judge put his glasses back on, scribbled furiously, and handed a note to his assistant.

"Mr. Stewart, at this point I have not imposed or required any conditions of release. I advise you that *after* release conditions are imposed by this court, any violation of the conditions may result in your arrest, a higher bond may be required, and additional release conditions may be imposed. Any failure to appear at trial or hearing may be cause for you to be charged with the additional offense of bail jumping, a felony offense punishable by up to ten years at a Montana State Prison, and a fifty-thousand-dollar fine, in addition to any consequences imposed for the pending charged offenses. Any bond you have posted may be forfeited. Do you understand these terms?"

Lucius said, "Yes, sir, I do."

"There is to be no contact with the victim. You are hereby remanded to the custody of Emma Horserider, whom I see standing in the back of the courtroom with—is that a pug?"

Lucius and every head in the courtroom turned to look at the wriggling dog.

"She's a service dog in training, sir." Emma held Franny up to display a little red jacket emblazoned with the words 'Emotional Service Dog.'

The judge suppressed a smile, cleared his throat, and glared at Lucius. "Emma Horserider will be personally responsible for you, Mr. Stewart. If you do anything to violate any of these release conditions, you will get not only yourself in trouble, but also this fine upstanding member of our Billings community whom I know and trust. Do you understand?"

"Yes, sir." Lucius swallowed a lump in his throat. "Thank you, sir."

"Ms. Horserider, please see the clerk of the court for putting up the bail money." He paused. "And, Mr. Blackfeather, I hope you'll be in town long enough to make it to this man's trial. He's going to need your legal expertise. Don't go flying away on him, now, you hear me?"

Bert smiled. "I'll be sure to be here, sir. I've taken some time off from Homeland to be with my family. If it pleases the court, in keeping with my client's right to a speedy trial, we'd like to get on the court calendar as soon as we can."

"Rushing things a bit aren't you?" Judge Williams frowned. "You'll need time to build a defense, and the county attorney will need time to build his case against your client."

Miller responded a little too loudly, "I'm ready *anytime* Mr. Blackfeather is."

"Gentlemen," the judge remonstrated. "I won't allow this courtroom to be a competition to see who the better word-wrangler is. A man's life is on the line. Don't forget that."

Lucius whispered to Bert, "Do I go with you now? What do I do?"

Bert shook his head and spoke in a low voice, "Today they'll take you back to the detention facility, and your discharge paperwork will be put into motion.

You'll sign your release papers and the officers will see if you have any outstanding warrants. Tomorrow, or more likely the next day, when all your paperwork is completed, you'll be brought to the booking area, you'll change back into your own clothes, and then you'll be released. Emma and I will be waiting outside to pick you up."

The judicial assistant handed the judge a note. "Says here, we will see you back in court first thing in the morning eight months from today. Sorry, gentlemen, that's the speediest trial you're going to get in Yellowstone County. Too many cases, not enough judges. Count your blessings you're not in New York City. Cases can take two years to get to trial." He slammed the gavel down. "This matter is adjourned."

Chapter Twelve

When Lucius walked out of the detention facility and crossed the street, the megawatt grin on his face kicked Tallulah's pulse up a notch. He embraced Tallulah, shook his "cousin's" hand, and rubbed the pug's belly.

"Thanks for getting Tommy and Jimmy to watch out for me, Bert. Nobody troubled me last night." He stood and glanced between Emma and Bert. "One of you want to explain how we're related?"

Emma threw her arms around Lucius. "Nice to meet you great-great-grandfather."

Emotions raced across the man's face. Lucius frowned in puzzlement, smiled, then blinked back tears, his throat working spasmodically. Tears welled up in her eyes, and she didn't bother to wipe them away. This event, this change in status, going from alone and lonely, to being embraced by a large family would be overwhelming for anyone, much less a man who had been in limbo for a century. She walked over to the grass with Franny, away from the family circle.

"Tallulah, where do you think you're going?" Bert called.

She thought she was being subtle. *Apparently not.* "Just wanted to give you guys a little privacy."

Bert waved her over. "We need to talk." When she drew closer, he lowered his voice, "Lucius needs a shower and clean clothes. And we need someplace to chat—without video surveillance cameras watching our every move." He tilted his head at the cameras on the outside of the detention facility.

Tallulah stepped back and gave Lucius a once over. "Will's about the same size as Lucius—except for the belly. Until we can get to a clothing store, I bet we can find some jeans, a shirt, and a belt he can borrow back at the hotel. There's a freezer full of bison burgers and buns in the kitchen. We could talk there too."

Bert stroked his chin. "Sounds like a plan—except for the fact that it's a crime scene."

"Well, I just gave you my one and only idea. You have a better one?"

"The only area Otterlegs taped up was the front door," Emma said. "There has to be another entrance."

"I thought your brother said it was crime scene?" Tallulah asked. She made air quotes with her fingers. "As in, 'Do Not Enter.' "

Bert put his index finger to his lip. "Shhh. Big Brother is watching."

Glassy-eyed, Lucius appeared to be in a daze.

Tallulah waved her hand in front of his face. "You okay, big boy?"

"Okay? I'm more than okay. I'm fine as cream gravy." The glassy-eyed stare morphed into a face-splitting grin. "I have a family. I struck gold in the outhouse."

Bert roared with laughter and slapped his thigh. "I guess you could say you found a pony in the pile of manure that's been your life."

Franny danced and yipped, running in circles around Tallulah and Lucius, binding them together with her leash.

Tallulah smiled. "Did you train her to do that, Emma?"

"Pretty smooth, but no, she did it all on her own." Emma motioned to her pickup truck. "Why don't you two ride with me? If they left a deputy watching the hotel, I'll give Bert a call and we'll reevaluate our plan."

"At least I'll be able to get my rental car." She couldn't keep the car forever and at some point in time, she'd have to go back to New Jersey—even if she did want to see where things were going with Lucius.

After a thirty-minute ride, they arrived at the Hotel LaBelle, where no deputy sheriff kept watch over the place. "My guess is they'll send a guy out once a day to check on the scene, make sure no squatters move in." Emma shut the engine off and grabbed a large buckskin pouch off the backseat. "They're understaffed and, as you saw in court today, overworked."

Lucius led them to the back entrance.

Tallulah tried the door. "Locked."

"Not a problem." He picked up a rock and pointed at the bottom. "Will keeps a spare key in this fake stone."

Emma phoned Bert and directed him to park in the back lot near the ramp up to the porch.

Tallulah returned from Will's room with clean clothes, soap, shampoo, and towels. "Pick a room, any room. I'll find us some lunch while you get cleaned up."

After pulling out six burgers and buns, she rummaged around through the jumble of utensils in the kitchen drawers and cabinets and wondered how Will could find anything in this mess. Drawer and pantry organizers would have been a good start. At last, she found a frying pan, flipper, and condiments.

Bert arrived, his briefcase on his lap. "Hope you can find us a beer to go with those bison burgers. I could use a brew after today's tour de force."

"Will said he had a lot of local ones on tap." She went out to the bar and returned with an empty glass. "Guess he didn't pay that bill, either."

"Water will have to do, then." Bert shook his head. "He really had no nose for business. What the hell was he thinking?"

Wet hair slicked back, Lucius strolled in at that moment smelling like soap. "Thank you. I feel almost human." He gave her a hug and slowly rocked back and forth.

Damn. He looked, smelled, and felt like hot sex on a stick.

Tallulah's face burned and not from the heat of the cooking range. She hadn't even turned it on yet. Maybe she didn't need to. She could probably cook the burgers with the temperature she generated every time she was near Lucius.

"I can tell you what he was thinking," Lucius kissed the top of Tallulah's head, released her, and pulled up a chair. "He gambled on a long shot—the success of this hotel—and he lost. He put the money in to fix it up but didn't count on the extras, like paying for repairs, cleaning, and keeping the lights on. Instead of selling and cutting his losses, he threw good money after bad."

Emma's face reddened, and she slammed her palm on the kitchen table. "It's not his to sell."

Bert pulled yellowed newspapers and legal documents from his leather case. "Your will gave everything to Mourning Dove and your heirs should you die before she did. So, it really belonged to your daughter, Snow Flower."

Lucius nodded. "Such a pretty name. I wish I'd met her."

"Beautiful Blackfeather tried to claim the hotel for your daughter when she turned eighteen. The bank claimed you never paid off the mortgage, so they sold the hotel to a pair of brothers."

"Why those horse thieving—" Lucius stopped. "I remember those two simpletons. They got drunk, argued over a woman, and shot each other."

"After you disappeared and the brothers died, most people around here considered the hotel cursed. The bank couldn't get anyone else to buy it, so it sat empty all those years."

Lucius ran his fingers through his hair. "Now what do we do?"

"Your heirs are sitting here with you," Bert said. "Will never had the right to buy the hotel. With the deed you gave to Tallulah, your last will and testament, and the wedding ring inscribed to Mourning Dove from you, we have a clear chain of ownership for Hotel LaBelle."

Tallulah's ears stopped working when she heard *wedding ring*. "Lucius?" Her heart hammered attempting to beat its way out of her chest.

He looked at her and smiled. "Yes, darlin'?"

He skipped over the wedding ring when he told her about the curse. Her voice came to her as if from the bottom of a well. "I thought you said she refused to

146

marry you?"

"She refused to marry me here in the hotel with a judge." He leaned back, tipping the chair on two legs. "Said the Crow didn't need a ceremony. I gave her mother a horse and a rifle. Among her people, that made us married."

Mouth dry as cotton batting, Tallulah turned away from the table and wiped a stray tear off her cheek. *The woman died over a century ago. Focus on the meals. Not the wedding ring.* The burgers sizzled, sending splatters of scalding grease on the range and her wrists. "Shoot!" She dropped the metal spatula into the iron pan with a clank. Arms encircled her waist, and she jumped.

Warm breath tickled her neck and a frisson of awareness shivered up her spine. "You okay, darlin'?"

"I'm fine." She struggled against Lucius' embrace and hoped she sounded more convincing than she felt. "Just trying to get food on the table without torching the place."

"Uh-huh." He grabbed the pan out of her hand. "Let me do this before you ruin the meat and give yourself more burns."

She twisted away from his other hand and busied herself getting everyone glasses of water. It wasn't fair. She cared for him, and she had thought the feeling was mutual. Yet, she heard the yearning in his voice when he spoke about Mourning Dove. He had unfinished business. Tallulah had no desire to play second fiddle to a dead woman. A living woman could never compete with a sainted ghost, not to mention a *child* he'd never met. As soon as they finished lunch, she would pack her dog up and leave for the East Coast. She slammed a glass down, and water splashed onto the table.

Bert shot her a questioning look and brushed water off his lapel.

"Sorry. My hand slipped." Appetite gone, Tallulah sat through the meal in silence. When everyone finished eating, she put the dishes in the dishwasher and wiped her hands on a towel. "My work here is done. You guys have a lot to discuss, so I'm going to head out now."

Three sets of eyes stared at her, and then they all spoke at once.

"You can't go!"

"What's wrong?"

"What the heck?"

Emma retrieved the buckskin bag and handed it to Tallulah. "Don't forget this. It's yours now."

Tallulah looked in the sack. "I really shouldn't. This belongs to your family." She removed the medicine stick and placed it on the table. "In fact, Lucius should keep this."

He cocked his head, reached over, and grasped the rod—and disappeared.

****

Lucius could see and hear them, but from the commotion Emma, Bert, and Tallulah were making, they couldn't see him. He dropped the medicine stick on the table, and a collective gasp of relief told him he was back.

Tallulah's rounded blue eyes reflected her fear. "Where did you go?"

"I think I slipped back into limbo." He placed his hand on the stick, and a surge of power raced up his arm. The world shifted sideways, blurred, grayed, and he found himself back where he never wanted to be again, between the living and dead.

This time no one spoke.

Removing his hand from the rod returned him among the living. "Don't that beat all? That thing still has lots of power left in it."

Bert eyed him like a buyer checking out a new horse. He lifted his chin. "Do it again."

Another century in limbo was not to his liking, not one bit. "Not sure that's a good idea. What if I get stuck?"

"I have a feeling that isn't going to happen," Bert said. "Humor me."

Lucius picked the rod up and shifted instantly. When he again dropped it on the table, his return to the living was faster, less jarring than the first two times.

Bert wrapped the stick with a cloth napkin. "Now touch it."

Lucius followed Bert's directive, but this time he remained present, among the living. He removed the napkin and lifted it again. Like a light switch. Pick it up, on, fade into the other realm. Hand off, he reappeared among the living. On. Off. On. Off. As long as he kept coming back, this was more fun than riding a bucking bronco.

"He's flicking in and out so fast, I'm getting a headache," Emma protested.

"You can stop now," Bert said. "Thanks for humoring me."

"Looks like Beautiful reversed the curse and gave you a gift." Tallulah mused. "I think she offered it as a penance for the time you lost with…" She couldn't say the other woman's name. It caught in her throat and squeezed the air out of her chest.

Lucius sat back in his chair. "If only there was a way to make a living with this."

"Funny you should say that." Bert pulled out a business card and slid it over to Lucius. "My division could use someone with your talents."

"Bert Blackfeather, JD, Director, Anomaly Defense Division, Homeland Security," Lucius read. "What's an anomaly and what's Homeland Security?"

Without sharing all the horrific details of 9-11, Bert brought Lucius up to speed about the terrorist attacks on the United States and beyond that to what the world had been dealing with in recent years. "My organization deals with unusual weapons and methods of attack. I'm always on the lookout for people with, shall I say, unusual talents. Tallulah has agreed to work with me on an as needed basis. I'm hoping you might consider taking an occasional assignment with me as an independent contractor, should circumstances arise where we need your—skills."

"If it means I get to work with Tallulah, count me in." He tried to catch her gaze, but she looked away. "I'm proud to help my country."

"Good, then it's settled." Bert pulled out some more papers and handed Lucius a pen. "We need to get you an identity. Could you please sign this document here, here, and here, and I'll get the wheels rolling."

"What do I use for my birthday? Folks don't seem to like it when I tell them the truth." Some things never change, he thought.

"Just subtract your age from this year's date and that's your new birthday." Bert pointed to boxes on the sheet of paper. "Write your real birthplace and we'll make sure your new birth certificate shows a Lucius

Stewart was born at home on that day. Your social security card will come to Emma's address. You're not really *real* without a tax identification number."

"You can do that?" Tallulah asked.

"I'm the director of a very special division in a very special agency. You'd be amazed at what we can do." He collected the signed forms and put them back in his case. "I'll get these faxed to Washington. The folks in documentation will take care of the rest. And we'll be sure you have a squeaky clean digital identity on the Internet once we get you cleared of all charges."

Emma pointed at her watch. "What's the game plan, bro?"

"I need to look at the area Will torched and take photos. What I don't understand is why the sprinklers didn't go off. It's required in all new hotel construction."

"I can tell you what happened." Lucius described how Will had disabled the system by emptying out the water. "He was drunk as a skunk and hell-bent on burning this place down."

"We need photos of the basement. Tallulah, would you do that? Use your phone and text me the pictures. Lucius, come upstairs with me."

"What do you want me to do?" Emma called after her brother.

"Help Tallulah," he yelled back.

Tallulah found a light switch at the top of the steps and flipped it on. The two women clumped down the stairs into the dank basement. "There's the sprinkler system." Water pooled in low-lying spots on the uneven concrete floor. A drain in the center of the room had siphoned most of it away. Emma pointed out the sign, and Tallulah snapped photos of the open spigot along with the pools of water on the floor.

"All done. Let's go." Tallulah turned to go back up the stairs, anxious to escape the hotel and Lucius' searching gaze. "I need to get on the road."

A hand grabbed her elbow. "Not so fast. Last night, you and Lucius were trying to figure out where your relationship was going. Now you can't wait to shake the dust of Billings off of your feet. What changed?"

"Mourning Dove." Just saying the other woman's name stabbed at her heart. "He still loves her. Can't you hear it in his voice? It catches each time he says her name. For him, her death is still fresh. He never knew he had a daughter. Now you and your brother call him grandfather. And he's only, what? Thirty-five? My timing is off by a hundred years."

Emma dropped her hand. "You sure about this?"

"I can't stay here and watch him yearn for another woman, even if she did die over a century ago. I can't compete with a ghost." As painful as it was to leave, it would be a hundred times more agonizing to stay and be forced to watch him long for his dearly departed day after day.

"Have you told Lucius?"

"Hard to have an intimate conversation with the two of us having been in jail on and off for the last twenty-four hours." She sighed. Emma had a point. She wouldn't like it if he disappeared without an explanation. "Any chance you and Bert could give us some time alone?"

Emma gave her a thumbs-up. "I have some errands to run in Billings, stuff to pick up for the fair. That'll take me at least two hours. I'll tell Bert to make himself scarce. Work for you?"

"Thanks for taking care of Lucius." Tallulah realized with a pang she was going to miss this place, these people, and their incredible kindness. Her apartment was cozy but a tad lonely. No big boisterous family gatherings. No bickering siblings. Her closest friend in Trenton was the Chinese food delivery guy. By comparison to the close-knit feelings in Billings, Trenton was a hollow shell, empty and devoid of personal connections.

"Isn't that what family's for? It's the place where you go, and they can't throw you out."

Tallulah smiled. "That's what my grandmother always said too."

"We wise women know." Emma pointed up the stairs. "I'll find Bert, give you some space."

Excitement, anxiety, and sadness fought for dominance in her aching chest—and the blues were winning.

Chapter Thirteen

After Tallulah waved goodbye to Emma and Bert, she stepped away from the kitchen door and hugged her elbows. Her stomach churned, and she was grateful she hadn't eaten much for lunch. Franny, on the other hand, had eaten at least a quarter of a pound of meat and now snored in the corner on a bed of dirty linens. "We need to talk."

"What's up, darlin'?" Lucius attempted to pull her into his arms.

Wriggling like a pug, she escaped his embrace.

Hurt crossed his handsome face, and his moustache drooped. "Did I do something wrong again?"

"No, it's not that." Tears threatened to spill down her cheeks, so she turned away. No need for him to see her weeping. "You—you need to have time to process everything that's happening to you."

"I don't understand. What's that got to do with you and me?"

"You still love her, don't you?" Better to get it out in the open. Not dance around the other woman in the room. "Mourning Dove. I hear it in your voice every time you say her name."

He came up behind her and wrapped his arms around her. His chin rested on the top of her head. "You're jealous."

"No, absolutely not." How could she be jealous of

a dead woman, for Heaven's sake? This wasn't high school. This was adulthood, and while she didn't feel like being an adult, she had no choice. "You've never had the opportunity to mourn her passing. It's still fresh for you."

His hug grew tighter, and his chest heaved against her back. "I had a hundred years, half of them in darkness with nothing but the stars, moon, howling wind, and wild animals to console me. If that's not enough time, I don't know what is."

She turned in his arms and pulled back to look into his eyes, those beautiful, warm brown eyes. "Grief has its own timetable, Lucius. When my parents died, I was a child, didn't know what was going on. But deep inside, there was this hole where my parents should have been. Over the years, my grandmother filled that space with her love. My parents are a memory, but every now and again, I see that little girl, the little me, and I cry for her."

"No one ever gets over the loss of a parent." Lucius shook his head. "I miss my mother every day."

A sob tore from her throat. "I can't replace Mourning Dove or your daughter. Your great-great-grandchildren are here for you. They want to help you, take care of you, and get through this strange time of your new life."

"I would never think you could replace another person. You're independent, sassy, strong, smart—all the things I love, wrapped up in a delicious, curvy package of wild blonde hair and big blue eyes." He put his index finger under her chin and lifted it. "Give me a chance, please?"

Voice hoarse, Tallulah croaked, "I have feelings

for—" and her words were cut off with a searing kiss that curled her toes. Heart thundering, breathless, she could barely think straight, much less speak. Her body was doing all the talking—as was his.

He slid his hands under her shirt and caressed her breasts. "Time for us to pick up where we left off the other night."

She husked, "I need a shower."

His voice hummed in her mouth, "Can I join you?"

Weak-legged, she nodded assent. He walked her backwards to the elevator, showering kisses on her forehead, eyes, nose, ears, and throat. Heat radiated from every pore of her body, and she began to undress in the elevator as he did. By the time they arrived on the second floor, his hands had caressed her nipples into aching rigidity. She wanted to explore every sensual curve and angle of his well-muscled body. Maybe it *was* too soon, but she didn't care. Emotions and hormones cascaded and tumbled with each touch, shoving her rational self out the door. His voice, touch, breath on her neck set her on fire. She yearned to be one with this intense, funny, brave man from another time.

He carried her to the closest room, pushed the door open with his elbow, and set her on her feet. "I'm not leaving this room until I've had my way with you." Still kissing her and walking backward, he led her into a bathroom with a claw-foot tub and shower and pulled her into the shower. He turned on the water and adjusted the temperature.

When they were both enclosed inside the shower, Tallulah closed her eyes as Lucius drizzled shampoo onto her hair, the floral bouquet blending with his manly scent in a heady mix. He massaged her scalp with long, slow, firm strokes and she relaxed, practically melting under his gentle touch. His fingers traced soap bubbles down her neck to the base of her throat, and rubbed lazy circles around her nipples.

She returned his caresses with increasingly firm strokes on his back, then his buttocks, and between his legs, soap bubbles rising up and bursting. He moaned as she fondled him, stilled her moving hand, and pulled her in for a long, hard kiss. Then he turned her around, placed her hands against the wall, and slid deep inside her aching center. His right hand pulled at her wet nipple, while his left fingers probed her hidden folds and found her shuddering bud. He stopped moving.

"What's wrong?" She panted and wriggled against him, wanting more.

"Nothing, darlin'. Just enjoying the moment." He held onto her until she couldn't take it any longer.

"Don't stop, please, don't stop!"

At last, he resumed his long, slow lovemaking; each stroke, each touch, driving her further up the spiral of passion until she climaxed and shuddered to a breathless halt. Weak-kneed, she leaned against the wall and gasped for air.

"I can't move," she said.

"Don't worry." He wrapped her in a towel, lifted her off her feet, and carried her to bed. Lucius placed her gently on her back, then opened the cloth. "You're beautiful all over, every inch of you." He hovered over her, his erection tickling her inner thigh. She arched her hips upward rubbing against him, inviting him in.

"Not so fast, darlin', I've got some other things in mind."

His lips were on her nipples, sucking and nipping them playfully, arousing her to greater heights. And just when she was about to cry out in frustration, he slid his mouth down to her belly, leaving a blazing trail of feathery kisses on her skin. Her legs fell open, and his tongue teased her, sliding over her lower lips and tangling with her throbbing nub of nerve endings. He stopped.

"Please," she begged. "More, please."

He slid his long fingers inside her hot core, probing for her pleasure spot, and rolled an aching nipple between his fingers at the same time.

"I adore watching your face while I make love to you."

A flush of heat rolled from her toes to her cheeks.

"Aw, don't be embarrassed, darlin'. You're so beautiful. You have the most expressive eyes, and I want to kiss your lips until they're tender from my touch. I love your breasts, your rosy nipples, your lush, womanly hips. I want to make you happy. I want to watch you when you—"

She plunged over the abyss of pleasure, grabbed her pillow, and screamed. His long fingers slid deeper inside her and played her like a violin, bringing her yet again to another series of trembling aftershocks of pleasure.

"I want you inside me." She gasped.

Lucius pulled himself up in the bed and plunged into her, filling her quivering void with his warmth and firmness. Her excitement rose with his panting breaths, each thrust bringing her closer to another drop off the cliff of pleasure to her own little death and her mind and brain exploded with stars.

Within seconds of her climax, he erupted within her, fell on top of her, and murmured, "Darlin' Dovie, I love you so much."

****

Lucius came out of his sex stupor with Tallulah pushing and clawing to get out from under him. "What's wrong?"

Tears streamed down her face, and sobs tore from her throat. "You. Me. Us. We're all wrong." She stormed out of the room, and he jumped up, trailing after her, admiring the swing of her fine bottom as she practically ran away.

"I don't understand." *What flew up her nose?* "I thought you wanted to go to bed with me. You tore my clothes off and threw yourself at me."

"You—you don't even know what you did, do you?"

"I made sweet love to a wildcat, and I was looking forward to some more." Was she always this crazy after sex? Taming broncos had to be easier than this. "Don't you want to do it again?"

"Get away from me. I'm not going back to bed with you now, or ever."

"You mean you didn't *like* it?" He could have sworn she'd enjoyed it as much as he had.

She stood in the elevator, grabbing her clothes, throwing his in his direction. "Like it?" She laughed. "No, I didn't *like* it. I *loved* it. It was the *best* sex I've ever had in my *life*."

"Tallulah, darlin', I don't understand. If you like splitting the sheets with me, that's a good sign. We're meant for each other."

Yanking up her pants and pulling her shirt over her

head, she hopped faster than a cat on a hot tin roof. "You didn't see me. You saw *her*. Every kiss, every moan, every freaking thing you did, you were thinking about *her*."

The woman was plumb loco. "Tallulah, I—"

"Don't you Tallulah me. Not after you called me her name. Not after you called me 'Dovie.'"

Stunned, his feet went out from under him, and his tailbone hit the hardwood floor with a thud. "I did what?"

"Yeah, you don't even remember doing it, that's what makes it sincere. You had sex with me, but I was just a stand in for the woman you really love." She pulled her boots on and shouted, "Franny, where are you, baby? Time to go."

The brass door to the elevator clanged shut, and she hit the button hard. The box began to descend along with his heart. *She's leaving me.* The first woman in a hundred years to make him feel alive and he ruined it with the name of a woman long dead. He banged the back of his head against the wall and howled.

****

Tears and snot streaming down her face, Tallulah wiped her nose with the back of her sleeve and hit the gas. She'd burn the shirt when she got home along with every other piece of clothing that smelled of him. "I'm such an idiot. I should have seen this coming a mile away, but he sucked me in with those big, sincere brown eyes and his soft lips." She slammed the steering wheel with the heel of her hand. "Damn him!"

Franny whined, and she lowered her voice. "I'm sorry, baby; I'm not mad at you. I'm angry at myself. Fool me once, shame on you—fool me twice, shame on me." Never again. She was done with men. Between the lying, thieving cheats like Will and the clueless ones like Lucius, she never caught a break. She needed time off from love and all the insanity that went with it. Hormone-addled brains didn't lend themselves to logical thinking. Lucius had just ripped the wound wide open. She was done.

"I'm done with men, Franny." She glanced at the pug, then back at the road and swerved to avoid a horse and rider that appeared on the side of the road out of nowhere.

"What the hell?"

Tallulah glanced in the rearview mirror. Nothing. Not even a horse or a dog, much less a rider. Trembling, her hands slick on the wheel, she took deep breaths and focused on the road ahead.

"I'm exhausted and distraught, that's all. I'll stop in Billings, stay at a decent hotel, and get on the road early in the morning." Just a few miles more and she'd be back in town.

She crested a hill and hit the brakes.

A Crow woman dressed in an elk-tooth-covered dress stood in the middle of the road, holding the reins of a blue roan covered with a colorful blanket.

Legs wobbly, Tallulah put the car in park and left the engine running. She stepped down from the SUV and approached the Indian woman.

The horse flicked his ears and neighed softly. A fly buzzed in the hot dusty air. The woman stroked the horse's muzzle and spoke to him in soothing tones.

"Are you lost? Do you need help?" Tallulah asked.

The woman laughed a high, bright sound reaching to the heavens. "No," she hand signed. "You need my help."

"Me? I'm fine." So strange, this woman on her own out in the middle of nowhere. "I'm not lost. I have a GPS."

An annoyed look crossed the other woman's face, and she shook her head so hard, her braids flew around her shoulders. "Go back."

"I *am* going back. I'm going home to New Jersey. Getting away from this land and all the craziness and ghosts and visions—" Tallulah gasped and put her hand over her mouth. "Omigod. You—you're a spirit—"

"My time on earth is over. It is time for him to live again. My mother forgave him."

Her legs threatened to buckle beneath her. Tallulah backed up to the car and leaned against it.

"You're Mourning Dove."

The spirit nodded.

"He's not over you," Tallulah said. "He loves you, and no one else will ever take your place. It's not your call. It's up to Lucius to learn to let go, and neither you nor I can control him."

Mourning Dove shook her head, mounted her horse, pressed her heels into his flanks, and disappeared.

Chapter Fourteen

Two weeks after his discharge, Lucius leaned on the gate and admired the way his new granddaughter— too many greats to mention—guided the skittish gray stallion around the corral, all the while, speaking to it in Crow. He had no idea what she said, but the horse named Steel seemed to understand her just fine. He shook his head and trotted slower with each turn. At last he stopped and stood still.

He knew just how Steel felt. Last week, he'd been introduced to his entire clan of living descendants at the Crow Fair. In preparation, Emma had provided a cover story. "You're a long-lost relative, you just found us through SearchMyFamilyTree.com and you came in for the fair."

He wondered if Jimmy and Tommy would be at the pow-wow. "And got arrested?"

"Hey, a criminal record *really* makes you part of the tribe. Native Americans are arrested twice as often as whites for the same crimes and go to prison over a third more than the rest of the population in the United States." She brushed a piece of straw off his shirt. "Don't worry. We're all family here."

Corralled by a circle of people, some in war dress for the competitions, some in Indian princess clothing for the parade, and still others in jeans and chambrays, Lucius felt as jumpy as that horse. At last, one of the teasing cousins, someone in Emma's generation on her father's side, came over, slapped him on the back, and handed him a beer. Later on, he found a sign on his back in Crow. Emma translated it for him. "Kiss me." No wonder every woman—and a couple of men—at the fair had kept running up and pecking him on the cheek.

"Just remember who did it," she said with a laugh. "You get payback. That's what teasing cousins are for."

The fair ended, the teepees were folded up, the relatives scattered back across the western states, and Emma returned to her training business. She now approached Steel with soothing tones and put her palm out. He nuzzled at the treats and snorted. Steel belonged to Judge Williams, which showed his good taste in horseflesh and horse whisperers. Training consumed most of Emma's time, and Lucius mucked out the stalls, watered, and fed the great creatures with pleasure. Itching to be useful, he felt needed when he cared for the animals. Hardworking Emma reminded him of Mourning Dove and her industrious nature. Always looking for an opportunity, always sharing with her clan, always loving, his wife epitomized the best in his past life. His dead wife. He shook his head. *She's not here, buddy.* No matter how hard you look for her, she's not here. She's gone to the camp beyond. *Tallulah was alive and cared about you, and you drove her away.*

Emma came over to the fence, Steel trailing behind her, nudging the horse trainer's shoulder for more treats. "Want to take him back to the barn?"

"Looks like he's sweet on you. Not sure he'll let me."

"He needs to get used to other people. Don't worry.

He won't nip—not *hard* at any rate." She grinned, and just like that, she was the image of Mourning Dove.

"When you joke like that, you look just like your great-great-grandmother." He touched her cheek. "She had a wicked sense of humor and used to poke fun at me all the time."

"She learned well from her teasing cousins." She handed him the reins and began to unlatch the gate. "Here you go."

Steel snickered and shook his mane.

"Aww, don't worry, baby, he's family. *Old* family." She winked at Lucius.

A car horn honked as Bert's van appeared in a cloud of dust.

He rolled his window down and shouted, "Get in the van. Wellington woke up!"

"Judge said I'm not supposed to have contact with the victim."

"That was before. Now, Otterlegs wants to see if Will identifies you as his attacker."

He handed the reins back to Emma. "For Pete's sake. What about those boys Tallulah found? I thought the Sheriff issued an arrest warrant for them."

Bert motioned for him to get in the van. "He did."

"Why isn't Otterlegs going after them?"

"Bird in the hand is worth two fighting interstate extradition, my friend."

"I sure hope Will doesn't decide to send me up the river." Lucius shook his head. "I saved that dirty skunk's life."

"Gonna be hard to prove. Let's just hope he comes clean, tells the truth for once in his life."

Lucius shook his head and climbed in.

"Rattlesnakes don't change their tune."

Bert hit the gas.

Thirty minutes later, they sat in the lobby of Saint Vic's waiting to be escorted up to Will's room. Used to be, doctors came to a person's home, made house calls. Before Beautiful banished him to limbo, the town leaders invited him to serve on a committee to plan a hospital. With his hotel expertise, he was able to give them advice on how to build the rooms and what to include in their linen and cleaning inventory. He never imagined it would look anything like *this* glass and metal space with hard tile floors.

Visitors signed in at the front desk, asked for directions and wandered off with a dazed look on their faces. Employees with identification badges in long white coats and blue outfits that looked like loose pajamas strode purposefully past him. A few stopped by to say hello to Bert, surprised to see him in town. Each time, he introduced Lucius as his long-lost relative, coming back to Billings to settle down. Not a single person questioned the story. Any friend or family member of Bert or Emma was a friend of theirs, it seemed—except Otterlegs.

"That little man has it bad for me. I can see it in his eyes."

"Short man complex," Bert explained. "Speak of the devil, here he comes now."

The bantam rooster swaggered over to Lucius. "You. Come with me."

Bert waggled a finger. "Ah, Deputy, you know the rules. Wherever he goes, I go."

"Like a shadow," Otterlegs sneered.

"Exactly. And, just like Lamont Cranston, I know

what evil lurks in the hearts of men."

Who's Lamont Cranston? Lucius wondered if it was the name of another family member.

"Whatever." Otterlegs turned and led them to a bank of doors. "They transferred Mr. Wellington from ICU to a medical floor. He's very alert and oriented, according to the doctors, perfectly competent to identify his attacker."

The bell rang and they stepped into the elevator. Otterlegs jabbed at the sixth-floor button.

"You mean Wilson, don't you? Wellington's an alias."

Lucius wondered what his lawyer was up to with this strategy. Seemed a bit like poking the bear.

Otterlegs squirmed and stared ahead at the numbers. "We are aware of that."

"He has a record as long as your arm. Money laundering, tax evasion, irregularities with his fees for his check cashing business—"

"We know," Otterlegs snapped. "What's your point?"

Bert smiled. "Will—or whatever his real name is—has warrants out for his arrest in four states. You must really want the Sheriff's job if you're willing to take his word."

The deputy snarled, "If your client's innocent, you shouldn't be worrying about that, now should you?" Otterlegs nodded to the uniform sitting outside the door and entered the room.

Bandages on his head, Will sat upright in bed. A woman with graying hair sat in a chair to the right, holding his hand. When the door opened, they stared at the visitors.

"Mr. Wellington, do you recognize this man?" Otterlegs pointed at Lucius.

Will shook his head. "Never saw him before in my life."

"Say something," Otterlegs ordered Lucius.

"Hello." Lucius stopped speaking when Bert poked him in the leg.

Will shook his head. "Like I just told you. Never seen him before."

"Get closer to the bed, Stewart. He can't see you that far away."

Lucius looked at Bert for guidance.

Bert nodded. "Let the record show my client is being cooperative."

Lucius stepped to the side of the bed, opposite from the woman whose lips thinned.

"You know him now, don't you?" Otterlegs insisted.

The woman spoke up, anger simmering beneath her civil words, "Deputy, you know my husband isn't feeling well. You're not helping. He *said* he doesn't know the man."

Lucius and Bert exchanged surprised glances. *Will had a wife?*

"Mrs. Wellington," Bert said softly. "I believe I know who attacked your husband. Would it be okay if I showed some photos to both of you?"

"Well, okay, I guess—as long as you don't take too long. Honey, is it okay with you?"

Will nodded and motioned for Bert to hand him the phone.

Lucius glanced at the thug's pictures as he passed the phone over to Will. "Those are some mean-looking highway men."

Will took one look at the mug shots and what little color he had drained from his face. "That's them. Those are the men Vinnie sent to beat me up because I couldn't pay the vig."

Bert smiled. "Will you be willing to testify to this in court?"

Will nodded and handed the phone back. "Those two broke my fingers." He held up a cast encased hand. "They should pay."

Otterlegs stamped his feet like Rumpelstiltskin. "You're lying."

Mrs. Wellington pointed at Bert. "You a lawyer?"

"Yes, ma'am, I am."

"A very good one," Lucius added with a note of pride. *Family ties don't get much better than this.*

"Would you be willing to represent my husband?" She opened her purse and pulled out a checkbook. "How much do I need to give you for a retainer? My mother passed recently, which is why I've been away from my husband, taking care of her and then her estate. We aren't millionaires, but we do have money to pay you."

"Hand me a dollar."

Mrs. Wellington pulled a buck out of her pocket and handed it to Lucius, who passed it along to her husband's new attorney.

Bert grinned and jerked his thumb at Otterlegs. "Time for you to leave."

Otterlegs sputtered, "What the h—"

"Attorney-client privilege, you know the rules."

Lucius opened the door. "Don't let it hit you on the way out."

The only thing that would make today better is if Tallulah were here.

****

The phone rang for the hundredth time. Tallulah let it roll into voicemail. Again. She had zero desire to speak to anyone in the *entire* state of Montana—much less anyone from the Billings area code. Sure, she was happy to hear all the charges against Lucius were dropped, and he'd been exonerated. But why didn't he phone and tell her himself instead of having Bert and Emma call?

In place of the telephone, over the course of the past six months, Lucius had discovered the Internet, email, and social media. For a man who had no experience with computers, he learned fast. His first email to Tallulah came through her blog on the day she posted about her trip to Montana and the historic Hotel LaBelle—minus the drama.

Lucius wrote that Will bought the hotel with cash he borrowed from a mobster and put it in his *wife's* name. When the mobster threatened to kill his wife if Will didn't hand over the hotel in lieu of the money owed, he tried to torch it. Bert became Will's lawyer, and the wife didn't want the hotel and all the work that went with it. She sold Bert the hotel for a dollar to cover legal costs. All of which avoided lengthy probate court battles. The hotel was back in the family, and Lucius was the manager.

Tallulah let out a long sigh. *All's well that ends well...except for the little matter of still having pangs in her chest every time she thought about Lucius.*

Emma or somebody else must have helped Lucius with the Hotel LaBelle website. The vision of Lucius hunting and pecking at a keyboard to write and send an email, much less build a website, made her giggle. Once the website went up, his emails became requests for her professional assistance. Nothing personal, all business, she thought with a sour taste in her mouth. Tallulah provided feedback on the website and recommended setting up a page on Facebook, along with other social media sites to drive business to the hotel.

Facebook.

She should have never suggested he join that site. Tallulah shook her head. Based on her observations, it appeared he spent hours each day posting photos of the hotel and stalking her.

It began small. "Thanks for accepting my friend request."

The next day, he posted a photo of a mule deer herd drinking from the river on her page. "See any mules you like?" he asked.

No, she thought, your face isn't in that crowd.

Each day for the last three months, he posted photos on the page for the Hotel LaBelle and shared them on her page. Mountains, goats, wild turkeys, the river, trees and foliage, Emma's horses, and people she assumed were his new family members. Tallulah saw each post as a not so subtle reminder of how much he loved Mourning Dove, not her.

His posts were cheerful. The hotel was thriving.

That was a good thing, right? She should be happy for him. So why did she spend so much time crying?

Each time she clicked on the browser, she told herself she wouldn't go to Facebook to see if he posted anything new on her page. She didn't want to be his

Facebook buddy, she wanted to be with him, to be the woman in his new life. But, that could never happen. Not with Mourning Dove in bed between them. Never again.

I should delete him as a friend. Block him. Stop torturing myself with this "friends not lovers" relationship.

Each time she went to hit the "Unfriend" button, she stopped.

This being noble stuff hurt.

Franny yipped and danced at the door. "Time to go out? Okay."

Still in her pajamas, her favorite work wardrobe, Tallulah knew she looked like a bag lady. Of course, she didn't actually need to get dressed since the grocery store and the Chinese restaurant delivered. Plus, no one came near her when she took the dog out, not even the obnoxious, round man with the garlic breath who used to try to force hot dogs onto her pudgy pug.

Score one for the homeless look.

She opened the door and nearly fell over Bert.

"What are *you* doing here?"

"When an employee doesn't answer my voicemails, I get concerned." He rolled away from the door. "Going somewhere?"

"Ha! Good one. Just taking Franny out for a walk. Go on in; make yourself at home. We'll be right back."

While Franny examined every cracked piece of concrete, beer can, and disgusting piece of trash within reach of her flat nose, Tallulah ran potential scenarios through her mind.

He called me his employee, so he must need me for a remote viewing.

The thugs are being moved to Montana, and he wants me to go there to identify them.

Lucius sent him to beg me to come back.

She liked the last scenario the best but would have preferred Lucius to do the begging.

"Come on, Franny."

The bowling ball of a man approached with a hot dog package in his hand.

"For Heaven's sake, mister, if I've told you once, I've told you a hundred times, my dog does not need snacks."

He looked at her with surprise. "Your dog? These are for me." Shaking his head, he muttered something about nutty bag ladies and huffed past her leaving a cloud of garlic behind.

"Time to go inside, Franny." Still cringing with embarrassment, she pressed the up button and took the elevator to her floor. "We're back." She unhooked Franny's leash, and the pug flew to Bert's side, jumping up and down at his legs. "Coffee?"

He nodded. "Sounds good. Come here, little girl, I've missed your personality." He lifted Franny onto his lap.

"Your clothes will be covered in pug hair." She poured two mugs of steaming coffee and set a plate of oatmeal raisin cookies down along with an insulated carafe. "I'll give you a pet roller before you go."

After Tallulah moved three piles of unread mail, each mound topped with a sticky note with a receipt date, from the kitchen table, she and Bert dunked their cookies in silence. A raisin plopped into his cup.

"I suppose you want to know why I'm here."

"You wanted to tell me in person about the Crow

Fair and how Emma's horses won all the relays?"

"It was great. All the relatives got together and met Lucius. He was pretty overwhelmed by the size of his family. At the pow-wow, there must have been over a hundred people who could trace their lines back to Mourning Dove and him. Of course, we didn't tell them that. Just that he was a long-lost relative. I'm sorry you didn't stick around to see everything. You would have enjoyed it, especially the day we demolished Otterlegs." He finished his coffee and reached for the carafe to pour himself another cup. "And, yes, the horses Emma trained did well. Got any other guesses as to why I'm here?"

"What is this, twenty questions? Well, aside from the fact that you said you were worried about your employee—who, by the way, has received no W-9 forms from Homeland Security—I suspect your visit might be related to Lucius?"

"He misses you very much. Emma tells me he mopes around half the day, waiting to see when you're on Facebook."

So he was stalking her. It tickled her to hear this, but she kept a poker face.

"Why doesn't he call me?"

His eyes bored a hole in her forehead. "We have been. Your phone keeps rolling to voicemail."

"Not you, not Emma. Him. He can talk, and he can call me himself." She fumed. "What makes him so stubborn? Why won't he use the phone?"

"Why don't you call and ask him?"

"I'm not the issue. He's still in love with Mourning Dove." She flicked tears off her cheek "Besides, I— I've been busy."

"Doing what? He glanced around the room. "Posting sticky notes and collecting cereal box tops and dust bunnies?"

Tallulah glanced around the apartment. Dirty cereal bowls teetered in crooked stacks in the kitchen sink, the mail sat in an unopened pile, and her appearance—well, *perhaps* he had a point.

"I'm finishing a book, been working on it for three years." There. She said it. The book of her heart had been dormant, but when she came back to New Jersey, she knew she had to finish it and take a risk.

He leaned forward. "And letting the world go by?"

"Yeah, kinda. Franny's fine, as you can see. I have my priorities straight."

"You know what I think? I think you're hiding from your feelings." He sipped his coffee and watched her face.

"Wow. You must be psychic. Of course I'm avoiding them. Just the sound of Emma's 'Hiya!' forces me into a spasm of tears."

"He's pretty miserable."

"So am I, but you don't hear me whining."

He stared at her for one, two, three heartbeats.

"Okay, maybe I am. But this isn't about me. It's not about Mourning Dove, either." She described the incident on the highway during her retreat from the hotel. "She told me she wanted him to move on. He didn't get the message."

"You sure about that?"

"I'm pretty sure that when a man calls me by the name of another woman right after making love to me, he's not quite over her."

Bert looked down at the table and bit his lower lip.

"Point taken."

She wiped her nose with a paper towel. "So you have work for me? Or do I have permission to continue my writing?"

"Actually, I do. Can you dim the lights, and close your eyes?"

She turned off the lights and sat in a comfortable chair.

"I want you to think about the Hotel LaBelle—and go there."

Her eyes snapped open. "That's not fair."

"Humor me."

She closed her eyes again and thought about the mountains, the sky, and the river near the hotel. In seconds, she was over the hotel, looking down at the big wraparound porch. A man sat in a rocking chair looking at the river. *Lucius.* In his hand, he held a photograph. Her heart tripped and stumbled. She had to get closer, needed to see the picture. She zoomed in for a better look.

Choking back tears, she said, "Are you trying to make me hurt more than I already do?"

Bert's mouth dropped open. "I don't understand. What did you see?"

"Lucius holding a photograph of Mourning Dove—and crying."

Chapter Fifteen

WBOO Radio Station, New York City
One Month Later

Tallulah adjusted Franny's little red vest and made sure the little pug was settled into her bed in the studio before putting on the headphones. Despite the soundproofing in the glass enclosure, the *On Air* sign in the outside lobby alerted studio visitors a live show was in progress and to minimize the background noise. The "Ghost Radio Hostess with the Mostest," Brooke Hallows, gave her the thumbs-up and wrapped up a commercial for an electronic voice phenomena recorder preferred by nine out of ten ghost hunters. She cued up her signature wailing violin and spooky music and rolled into her introduction of her new guest.

"I'm excited to introduce this evening's guest to you. Please welcome author, ghost hunter, and hotel inspector, Tallulah Thompson. You may have heard about her exploits about a year ago when she removed both a pesky spirit and a fraudulent innkeeper from one of the oldest hotels in Montana, the historic Hotel LaBelle. Tonight, she's here to tell us about her latest adventures and to talk about her best-selling book, *Haunted Hotels Across America*. Tallulah, could you tell my listeners a bit about yourself and what prompted you to write this book?"

"Yes, I'd be delighted to." The book of her heart, the stories of her life helping spirits move on, had been her top secret project for the last three years. Her grandmother's admonitions combined with her lack of confidence about putting her book-baby out for the world to see—and criticize—had kept it under wraps. After Lucius and Hotel LaBelle, however, she knew it was time to go public and publish. "First off, I want to thank you for having me on your show, Brooke. I've been an avid listener over the past year, so it's a thrill to be here with you and your wonderful fans. They always ask the best questions!"

"Yes, they do." Brooke winked at her. "Never a dull moment."

"I'm going to give your audience a bit of background on me. My grandmother was a Choctaw Medicine Woman."

"Excuse me," Brooke interrupted. "Could you elaborate on that?"

"Yes, of course. The Choctaw Nation is a Native American Tribe that farmed Oklahoma before Americans and Europeans arrived on the scene and forcibly removed them from their lands over the course of the Trail of Tears."

Brooke frowned, shook her head, and motioned to move along.

"My grandmother was a gifted healer and could see the spirits of those who had passed on. In her time, this was considered a great blessing. People from all over came to ask for her help."

The phones were starting to light up with calls. The hostess-with-the-mostest smiled and said, "So you're carrying on her work?"

"Yes, but it took me a while to accept my gifts." Tallulah paused. "My mother also saw those without bodies, what we call ghosts or spirits, but that resulted in her being put in a psychiatric hospital and heavily medicated. Modern medicine thought she was hallucinating."

"Okay, bring us up to speed." Brooke rolled her index fingers over each other. "When did you decide it was time to enter the realm of paranormal work?"

"When I realized that I would never be whole until I embraced my heritage and my talents. I owe a debt of gratitude to an ancient Crow Medicine Woman and a man who died over a century ago. Together, they freed me from my greatest fear—being ridiculed or locked up because, as the cliché goes, I see dead people."

"Wow. What an amazing story. We're going to take a little commercial break, and when we come back, we'll talk about some of the ghost tales in your book, *Haunted Hotels Across America*, and take some calls."

Tallulah sipped her water while the promo for an upcoming paranormal conference played. "Am I doing okay?"

"Oh, you're great, a real natural. Just steer clear of the Debbie Downer stuff like the Trail of Tears and the crazy mother, okay?" She flashed a quick grin. "People listen to my show to be entertained, not educated."

Tallulah nodded. "I'll try to be more entertaining." *Heaven forbid I should educate people.*

The promo ended and Brooke went back into hostess mode. "We're here with author and ghost hunter, Tallulah Thompson, who is going to share some of her haunted hotel stories with us. Tell us, where are the most hauntings in the United States?"

"Great question, Brooke. I know New Orleans is right at the top of that list, along with Gettysburg, Baltimore, Galveston, Portland, Oregon, San Francisco, Chicago, Washington, DC, Athens, and Ohio, as well as Savannah, Georgia."

"A lot of paranormal investigators go to those cities." The host mouthed, *You're doing great* and gave her the thumbs-up.

"I think the residents of New Orleans are the most open and accepting of their spirit citizens. I was in an art store and the owner asked me what brought me to the city. When I told them I was called in to help the Crescent City Inn with a spirit that had a habit of pulling the sheets and blankets off guests while they slept, he asked me if I'd help them with the dead woman on the third floor where they stored the artwork. Apparently, she'd been murdered on the site and didn't know she was dead. I was able to help her go to the light, and the gallery owner was so happy, he gifted me with a piece of art." She laughed. "He had no idea the painting contained a particularly nasty spirit and I eventually had to get rid of it. That was one ghost who did *not* want to leave!"

"Let's take some callers." Brooke pressed a button, and her assistant gave her the listener's name and city. "We have Armand from Armonk on the line with us now. Armand, what's your question?"

"Yah," the man wheezed. "I been trying to figure out how you know you can get rid of these spirits?"

"Great question, Armand," Tallulah said. "I have a checklist of things I insist the hotel owner or manager do before I go in. First, they have to have the hotel inspected by licensed electricians, plumbers, and

HVAC professionals. I can't tell you how many times it turned out that the lights flickering mysteriously were really a short in the wiring."

"Ah, good point," Brooke interjected. "You're singing my song. Rule out the normal before you go after the paranormal."

"Exactly. Then I ask to stay overnight in the room with the most unusual activity."

"Oooh, creepy. Good stuff." The hostess broke into Tallulah's explanation, *again*.

"The majority of the hauntings are residual. Sort of like a video playing the same scene over and over, these phenomena are not interactive with living people. One of the most famous of these in America is Lincoln's phantom funeral train. Railroad workers saw the procession traveling nightly up the Hudson River, long after Lincoln was buried. Those can be addressed by putting a lot of electronic equipment, radios, TVs, computers, those sorts of items, into the space to break the infinity loop."

Brooke was drinking coffee, unable to interrupt.

"The ones I work with are people who have not passed on into the light. These spirits are unaware they are dead and will attempt to get the living's attention because they have unfinished business."

"So when ya sprinkle them with holy water, do they sizzle and burn like vampires?" Armand from Armonk queried.

"I have no experience with vampires. I just deal with earthbound spirits who need help moving on."

"What about werewolves? Do you use silver bullets and garlic on them?"

"Umm..." Tallulah beseeched Brooke with her

eyes. The one time the hostess didn't jump in was when she needed her.

Get me outta here!

"Vampires and werewolves are on my other show, 'Shapeshifters among Us.' You should save those questions for tomorrow night when we have Mary Rose Wiley, an expert on evil Djinn and Shadow People. Thanks for calling, Armand."

Tallulah looked at the digital read out. Only twenty more minutes. She hoped she sold some books. After three years of working on the manuscript, then putting it away for fear of going against her grandmother's advice, she'd finally finished and self-published. An immediate hit with fans of the paranormal, she'd been booked on blogs, interviewed by websites, and now was being invited to radio. Supposedly, Brooke had over ten million followers. If ten percent bought her book, she'd be richer than the queen of England.

"Chris from Columbus is with us. Chris, how are you tonight?"

"Annoyed," a man whined. "It took forever to get through tonight."

"Well," she soothed, "we speak almost every evening, don't we Chris?"

"Yes, but I like to be the first caller so I can ask the good questions first."

"Do you have a question for Tallulah?" Brooke rolled her eyes.

Tallulah guessed every talk radio show had a few like Chris.

"How much you charge for getting rid of hotel ghosts? I'm thinking if you can go after haunted hotels, I can go for the bed and breakfasts and youth hostels.

It's a niche market. I just need to know how much money I can plan on earning. My first case has gotta cover the five hundred dollars for the deluxe ghost hunting kit."

"I have a nondisclosure clause with my clients. I cannot discuss the names of the hotels or details of a consultation without their written permission."

"Ball park it for me, will ya?"

This guy's like a pit bull with lockjaw. He won't let go.

"It varies with the magnitude of the case, so I really can't give you a price. I *can* tell you at this point in my career, I don't leave my office for less than five thousand dollars, including travel expenses. Does that help?"

"Oh boy! I'm ordering that kit online now. Thanks!"

Brooke shook her head and smiled.

"Oh, we have another caller. Lou from Louisiana, you are on the air with our guest, Tallulah Thompson."

"Thank you." The decidedly male caller did not have a trace of a southern accent. "My hotel is haunted, and I need help."

Brooke nodded. "That's what we're here for, Lou. Tell us what's going on."

"I see her everywhere I go, can't stop thinking about her."

"How do you know it's a female?" Tallulah puzzled over the voice. Where had she heard it before?

"Oh, she's like flesh and blood, she's so real. Here one day, gone another. Tall, wild blonde hair, eyes that will strike terror into a man's heart." His voice dropped lower, and a flock of butterflies took flight in her stomach. "Wears a white flannel nightgown that shows all her curves."

Franny shrieked like a banshee, and Tallulah leaped to her feet to see what happened to her pug. The little dog dug at the door of the booth as if the tastiest bone in the world waited on the other side. Tallulah stared through the glass, and her heart thudded so loudly she was sure the entire WBOO listening audience could hear it.

Time and motion stopped, fused into this one instant. Forcing herself to remember to breathe, his magnetism drew her to him. Their gazes locked. Tearing up, she placed her palm on the glass and whispered, "Is it really you?"

On the other side where the *On Air* sign shone brightly, a weary looking Lucius Stewart leaned his forehead against the glass and whispered into his own itty-bitty phone.

"She haunts my days and nights. She saved my life one night, and then took it away." A mournful note crept into his voice, plucking at her heart. "I hurt when I inhale because her rose-scented perfume isn't in the air. I can't exorcise this spirit. When something good happens, I want her to be with me—but she's not there. I can't live without her, can't make my life's music. She's the violin to my bow. I have to have her at my side in real life. I can't stand the taunting memories, the ghost of the love of my new life. Can you *please* help me, Tallulah?"

His pleas tapped at the wall she'd built around her heart, the one made with tears and sorrow. Could she have a happily ever after with a man from another era? Was she fooling herself—again? Her breath came in ragged little gasps, she could barely breathe. "You're from different worlds, perhaps she thinks you can never truly be together."

"I can live in her world. I love her more than I love my hotel."

More than he loves his hotel? Hotel LaBelle had kept Lucius and Mourning Dove apart. He was willing to sacrifice his baby, his life's work, for Tallulah?

"Perhaps she's afraid she can't compete with another more important ghost."

"I made peace with the old ghost, sent her to her resting place, at last."

Brooke tapped her on the shoulder and glared at Tallulah. "My guest has a caller with a particularly pesky problem, doesn't he? We'll return after we pause for station identification and pay some bills."

Tallulah opened the door, and Franny leaped at Lucius. She pawed at his feet, her whole body and curlicue tail wriggling in joy.

Lucius reached for Tallulah and yanked her in for a long, hard kiss.

Breathless, she put her hands on his chest. "I saw you holding a photo of Mourning Dove; you were crying—"

"I was saying goodbye. Telling her I was moving on." He hugged her closer. "I'm ready now, Tallulah, please believe me."

Barely able to think coherently, she gasped and pulled away. "I don't understand. How did you find me here?"

He gave her a slow, sexy smile. "Well, ya know that old sayin' about teaching old dogs new tricks? I've learned a lot about cars, computers, and telephones. Did you know pretty much everything about everybody, including *me*, can be found on the Internet?"

"In that case, smarty pants, what took you so long?"

His searing kiss cut off her complaints.

He was here. With her. In her world.

Although she would never force him to give up Hotel LaBelle, his willingness to sacrifice his wants for hers made her head spin. And, more importantly, he'd made peace with his memories of Mourning Dove.

He loves me; he really loves me! And I love him!

Brooke yanked the door open. "The phones are going wild. Get Romeo in here. The chemistry between the two of you is scorching the airwaves. Listeners are clamoring to know *everything* about you two."

Tallulah white-knuckled his hand and shook her head.

"It's okay, darlin', I can't wait to tell everyone about how I'm the long-lost relative and namesake to the original 'Love 'em and Leave 'em Lucius,' the very same spirit you helped to move on to the next world."

No one would ever believe the truth—even among this radio show audience.

He placed the tip of his finger on her lips. "You have to promise me one thing."

She kissed his palm. "What's that?"

He pressed his forehead against hers and placed his hands on her waist. "Tell me you love me, and you'll never leave me again."

She released a long, slow breath. "Until death do we part?"

"And beyond, darlin', and beyond."

A word about the author...

After working in health care delivery for years, Sharon Buchbinder became an association executive, a health care researcher, and an academic in higher education. She had it all—a terrific, supportive husband, an amazing son, and a wonderful job. But that itch to write (some call it an obsession) kept beckoning her to "come on back" to writing fiction. Thanks to the kindness of family, friends, critique partners, and beta readers, she is now published in contemporary, erotic, paranormal, and romantic suspense.

When not attempting to make students, colleagues, and babies laugh, she can be found herding cats, waiting on dogs, fishing, dining with good friends, or writing.

You can find her at www.sharonbuchbinder.com

~*~

Paranormal Romance Guild Winner—Best Mystery/Thriller, 2012

EPIC's eBook Award Finalist—Romantic Suspense, 2014

Paranormal Romance Guild Winner—Best Historical Paranormal Romance, 2015

~*~

Other titles by Sharon include...

Kiss Of The Silver Wolf
Obsession
Kiss Of The Virgin Queen
Some Other Child